Published by Carpetless Publishing

ISBN: 9780993436925

THE AUTHOR

GR Jordan is a self-published author who finally decided at forty that in order to have an enjoyable lifestyle, his creative beast within would have to be unleashed. His books mirror that conflict in life where acts of decency contend with self-promotion, goodness stares in horror at evil and kindness blind-sides us when we are at our worst. Corrupting our world with his parade of wondrous and horrific characters, he highlights everyday tensions with fresh eyes whilst taking his methodical, intelligent mainstays on a roller-coaster ride of dilemmas, all the while suffering the banter of their provocative sidekicks.

A graduate of Loughborough University where he masqueraded as a chemical engineer but ultimately played

CRESCENDO!

An Austerley & Kirkgordon Adventure

G R JORDAN

American football, GR Jordan worked at changing the shape of cereal flakes and pulled a pallet truck for a living. Watching vegetables freeze at -40°C was another career highlight and he was also one of the Scottish Highlands' "blind" air traffic controllers. Having flirted with most places in the UK, he is now based in the Isle of Lewis in Scotland where his free time is spent between raising a young family with his wife, writing, figuring out how to work a loom and caring for a small flock of chickens. Luckily his writing is influenced by his varied work and life experience as the chickens have not been the poetical inspiration he had hoped for!

TABLE OF CONTENTS

Dedicated to Andy,
Your encouragement remains.

Chapter 1

Leaving The Asylum

His eyes fixed on the metal gate ahead and the bile caught in his throat at the sight of the man lumbering toward it. Never had Kirkgordon entertained the thought of seeing this broken figure again, let alone agreeing to babysit this most curious of cats. Too much had gone before. Too much had been lost. The light that had lit up his life for the previous twenty years had been all but extinguished. It was the price that he had paid for following this shambling hulk into the very gates of hell. Contemplating this moment on the banks of the Miskatonic that morning, Kirkgordon had not foreseen the sheer hatred which now welled up inside. His wife had left him, his kids saw Dad now only one week out of four and his friends had abandoned him, all because of the episodes that now plagued his existence. Only the deepest depths of faith had kept him sane enough not to be locked up alongside the figure approaching him, a resident of Arkham's finest secure facility for the mentally compromised. His fists were clenched tight, his chest fought for breath and his blood coursed wildly. He muttered the most bitter of welcomes to the hated demon emerging from the sanatorium.

"Austerley, we got work to do."

A large, black, clearly governmental saloon was waiting at the sanatorium gates with five men in attendance. The first was Kirkgordon, dressed in black jeans, black ankle cowboy boots, a greyish T-shirt and a black leather jacket. He was nearing forty and it showed on his hair, or rather what was left of it. Greyness had taken over much of it, due to the incident he said, not age. Kirkgordon was stocky but not particularly tall. While not out of shape, he didn't have the looks of Adonis. Yet, of the men there, he was surprisingly the most dangerous.

Beside him stood Lord Farthington of Her Majesty's most secret of services. A tall English gent adorned in the customary Savile Row suit, with a bowler hat and umbrella "just to keep the yanks honest". He sported a most stunningly twirled set of whiskers and an accent that spoke of nobility even when it swore. Looking like the finest of British fools, he was there to keep things in order. Kirkgordon had been introduced to Farthington through an old, long-forgotten contact. His own research had drawn a blank but his contact had filled in the detail.

Unseen mastermind of many conflicts and coups, Farthington was a man who liked to keep his hands from the dirtier side of life. Like a chess grandmaster, he enjoyed manipulating and coercing others by means fair or foul but distinctly non-physical. Now in his later years, he headed up one of the government's more covert organizations, one which looked into the strange and unusual but definitely alarming.

The other men were employees of the FBI: one senior field agent and two strongmen, apparently there to control any hotness that the situation induced. They were dressed in black suits, possibly for Lord Farthington's benefit, and the firepower they each carried was immaculately concealed by the loose-hanging jackets. The FBI men moved to flank the releasee as he approached the car. Farthington stepped forward to greet Austerley while Kirkgordon turned from them all to take his place on the passenger side at the front of the car.

Austerley was not small in stature, measuring some six foot, and was carrying some bulk despite his incarceration. Hiking boots went well with the combat trousers he wore but then his garb broke out into a confused mélange of Christmas reindeer jumper and green and white bobble hat. His hands were chunky and somewhat hairy, while his face looked harried to the point of abuse, jowls dropping like those of a dog.

Farthington thrust a cigarette toward Austerley, apologizing that they were "American", before brandishing a silver lighter. Austerley dipped awkwardly to light the gratefully received stick of tobacco. As he drew in his first taste of fumes, Kirkgordon uttered in guttural fashion that Austerley should get his "worthless arse" in the car. Jumping to Austerley's side, the Americans tried to encourage him into the car but he just turned around, leaned back on the car, and smoked slowly, deeply and passionately on his first cigarette in five years. Kirkgordon glowered. The fact that Austerley had positioned himself clearly in his line of sight via the wing mirror hadn't helped.

Farthington agreed that Austerley's posterior should position itself into the car sooner rather than later. At the agent's urging, the car was cruising away from the sanatorium a mere three minutes later. Silence dominated, unnerving the Americans, who would occasionally touch their firearms through their jackets as if some weapon-stealing gremlin was afoot. At first this went unnoticed by Austerley and the reverential quiet continued. But then the newly freed man caught a glimpse of the Americans' guns. The agitation slowly built up through a shaking leg, then involuntary movements in the shoulders, before a sudden cascade of manic shouts sent the saloon's occupants into a frenzy.

"Dammit! NO! Don't shoot! Them not me. They'll come. Shuggoth. Darkness!"

The driver spun off the road on seeing Austerley's flailing arms in the rear-view mirror. The beast was stirring. Farthington's cool exterior lost its calm and a worried frown crept across his face. Both of the Americans in the back leapt onto Austerley, trying to suppress him, as a wild strength born from fear surged through his body. The drawing of the driver's gun sent Austerley into even wilder hysterics.

"Put the guns down. Gentlemen, holster your weapons." Kirkgordon sounded calm but extremely pissed-off. When the driver failed to react he found his gun taken from his hands and watched the chamber and ammunition fall to the floor as separate entities. One of the other Americans responded by putting his gun in Kirkgordon's face. He would wake up ten minutes later to find caked blood around his nose and his weapon missing. The third American was a quick learner and while holding Austerley with one hand, dropped his weapon to the ground with the other. The car had stopped at Hill Street close to Hangman's Brook. Stepping out of the front seat, Kirkgordon reached in and extracted Austerley before leading him firmly but gently to a bench overlooking the brook.

"What was that?" Farthington had recovered his dapper attitude. Standing aloof from Austerley, he looked deep into the dispassionate face of Kirkgordon. The Americans had been left in the saloon.

"Guns. He hates guns." Kirkgordon spat on the ground.

"Guns. That's all. Just guns?" Farthington's eyebrows stood up like the orchestra at the end of a concert.

"Yes, he hates guns." Kirkgordon did everything but say Farthington was dumb. Too long in the tooth, the agent didn't take the bait.

"Okay, when you're ready."

"Leave him with me. It's safer. I understand him." Kirkgordon felt Farthington staring into the windows of his soul. Protocol was being weighed up against practicality.

"Fine. He's your responsibility. No fuss. No nonsense. Nothing in the papers. And no diversions. And I want him breathing when he comes back to me."

"If I wanted him dead, he'd be dead. But you've made that calculation already. So, let's have it. What do you want with a mental case and a washed-up former player?"

"It'll have to be in front of Austerley too. You both need to hear."

Chapter 2

Austerley's Musical

Know-How

Austerley stared at the slow-running water in Hangman's Brook. Sitting on a small wooden bench with pursed hands, he looked like he was throwing invisible bread to non-existent ducks when the occasional fits and starts from the incident hit him. Kirkgordon sat down beside him but could only stare off into the fields, barely acknowledging the nervous man beside him. Farthington was an old pro and produced a collapsible seat which he placed directly in front of the bench, imposing himself into the view of both men. The British agent, ready to deliver his orders, was keen that neither man misunderstand or ignore them. A curt cough focused their attention on him, and Farthington set off on an explanation devoid of humour or warmth. Luckily for him, the subject matter was enough to entrance the listening pair.

"Recently, gentlemen, it has come to my department's notice..."

"Which department is that?" interrupted a serious-faced Austerley.

"The one I work for, Mr Austerley. Now, recently we have come to notice a certain individual's preoccupation with trying to obtain particular manuscripts for some unknown purpose. Normally these proceedings would not cause undue alarm, but one of our sources believes that this individual is looking to pick up such manuscripts from a specific location which is normally not accessible to the general public. Our man trailed the individual and overheard certain details of the location. One detail was the place. The other detail was *when* the place would be there. Said place being in Moscow; specifically, Улица на пороге."

Austerley became agitated, looking all around him while not fixing on anything in particular. If his mind had had a steam whistle, it would have been calling all to clear the tracks ahead.

"Zahn! It's Zahn." Austerley beamed into the confused faces of his companions. The smile was short-lived and, aware of their total incomprehension of his revelation, he started to rebuke their petty minds. "Imbeciles, stuck out in this world, totally ignorant of all that goes on. And they lock *me* up, oh, dumb, mad old Austerley. One wonders how this place goes on. Intelligence services. Dressed-up clowns who can't do their job..."

"Austerley, shut it or I'll put you back down that hole personally!" Kirkgordon had taken particular offence at being lumped in with the "clowns".

"Yes, Mr Austerley, a degree of decorum, if you please. And also kindly elaborate on this Zahn fellow. Most intriguing." Farthington always cut through any nonsense to get to his answer. He was the money, the man who could pull the strings.

Austerley breathed deeply and prepared to speak slowly and simply to the children. "Eric Zahn. German viol player of extreme talent. It was said that he played either with or against the night creatures that visited his apartment. Certainly, in the normal world he was a remarkable musician, but he was once visited by a gentleman who took great fright from that which came to them one night. Said gentleman described music written in bizarre patterns and played in tones and notes from somewhere else."

Austerley had his shoulders hunched up now and was in full flow. With every passing detail the excitement across his face grew and the previously tired jowls visibly reddened with life. Farthington kept nodding in anticipation of the pertinent exposé, but Kirkgordon was sombre, pondering every word.

"One night he took fright from the apartment and was unable to find it again. Zahn was believed to have been either abducted or killed in the incident. Although a stunning musician, he was also a mute, so the true tales of what came to the apartment were never fully understood by anyone except Zahn himself."

Austerley stopped speaking and went back to staring intently at the brook. Farthington gave Kirkgordon a look which said: Is that it? A shrug of the shoulders replied: How should I know? There was a half-minute of calm and tranquillity with only the babbling of the brook. Then Kirkgordon's breath pulsed quicker and built like a string crescendo before the awaited outburst.

"And what does this have to do with anything?"

If incredulity could be delivered in a look then Austerley was a master postman. After dismissing Kirkgordon as clown number one, Austerley stared questioningly into the eyes of the British agent. Finding no response, generosity compelled him to elucidate for the feebler minded.

"Zahn lived at the Rue d'Auseil. This is an abuse of the French language, collapsing the original 'au seuil', translated as 'at the threshold'. The street is seen as being on the cusp of somewhere else. And 'Улица на пороге' is how they say it in Russian." Austerley, instead of glorying in his victory, became drawn. His face had lost its red glow and had turned a dull pale.

"What is it?" Farthington sensed the feeling of unease.

"Zahn is believed gone. Anyhow, he cannot tell anyone anything, being a mute, and one that was unstable in mind. So what do they want?"

"The music. It has to be the music." Kirkgordon was now standing, as if this enlightening of the audience signified his full emergence onto the academic scene.

"Of course it's the bloody music! But why?" Farthington snapped. Kirkgordon, chastised, sat down.

Austerley stared at the brook. After a few seconds he stood up and walked to the edge of the bank, deep in thought. Suddenly, he whipped his head round to stare at Farthington with a look of horror. The agent had seen enough people under extreme fear to recognise the look of hopelessness that was forming on Austerley's face.

"What, Austerley?" came the gentle whisper from the string-puller.

"The music either protected Zahn from the darkness that came, or he played with it, in a sort of malevolent orchestra. So, either someone wants protection from this darkness which means either it's coming very shortly or it's already here. Or, ..."

"They want to play with it," murmured Kirkgordon, "which means either it's here or they want to summon it!"

"Invite it, actually, but yes," Austerley corrected.

"So, either it needs to be stopped or it needs putting away. Whatever it is. Do you know what it is, Austerley?" Kirkgordon was rapidly regretting taking on his charge.

"No." Austerley shook his head slowly. "But if Zahn's music is involved then it's Elder. It's like before... Sorry." The two misfits stared at each other, caught up in the common bond of the damned.

"Gentlemen, it seems pertinent that you get to Russia and that you are the first to this threshold," Farthington ordered. "It seems that you do indeed have work to do."

Chapter 3

In-Flight Entertainment

The business jet was an extremely plush affair. Kirkgordon had never been in a Gulfstream V and at first he enjoyed the lavishness of the interior cabin. The arrival of a rather good-looking stewardess further enhanced his mood, although he did notice she had a discreetly holstered weapon. He thought using firearms on aircraft was rather risky and, given Austerley's earlier outburst, a degree of surprise that Farthington would allow such armament crept in. The matter played on his mind until he fully perceived the shape of the weapon and recognized it as a dart gun. The gamekeepers were watching the rhino.

Austerley was enjoying some rather fine wine. Kirkgordon didn't take in the vintage or vineyard it came from but then he wasn't actually listening to Austerley. He would nod his head occasionally but his mind was preoccupied. Two days ago he had been approached by one of Farthington's men in his quiet local.

He should have realized. The money was too good; the risk had to be high. But what really vexed him was the driving force behind his taking on this venture, a journey that was bound to take him back to that maddening fool who had gotten them into such a foul scrape underneath that accursed graveyard. Deep down he felt pity for Austerley. Something made him sympathetic to that blasted man. The things they had seen had bonded them together for better or, as it seemed now, for worse.

Farthington was quite engaged by Austerley. They talked deeply of wines and culture, about Russia and its current battles and problems. But what most fascinated Farthington were Austerley's days as a professor at Miskatonic University in Arkham. Strictly speaking, he had been Professor of Tribal History and Cuisine, but this was just a front. Austerley had been at the forefront of research into the Eldars. A walking encyclopedia of all things hidden in the deep, sent from outer space's blackest regions, or, indeed, scattered throughout our known world. It was rumoured that Austerley had obtained a personal copy of the dreaded Necronomicon, and when questioned by Farthington he did not seek to deny this truth.

The conversation continued gently enough until the mention of one name brought a slumbering Kirkgordon to life.

"Did you say Carter? Don't you even mention that name! You know where that took us last time." Kirkgordon pointed an accusing finger at Austerley. Sweat was beginning to break out on his head.

"You mean Randolph Carter?" quizzed Farthington.

"Randolph bloody mad mannish freak Carter! Yes, Farthington, that damned lunatic," said Kirkgordon.

"Oh, he was no lunatic..." Austerley interjected, only to have Kirkgordon round on him again.

"He jumped into clocks. Talked to cats. And went looking for the darkest presence ever known. He was one hundred percent lunatic. Top commander in the la-la-la crowd! What's worse is that we have his chief of staff sitting opposite us now. His problem is your problem. Is it dark? Yes. Is there something malevolent in the darkness? Yes. Can it drive us mad? Yes. To a point worse than death? Yes. Can we stop it? No. Oh, what the hell, let's take a good look anyway! Bloody lunatics."

Austerley went quiet and his face dropped down into his chest. Whenever he looked up, Kirkgordon's eyes enforced the silence. Farthington, not wanting an incident at forty thousand feet, stared out of the window at the white cloud landscape below and the piercing sun on the port side. Five minutes passed without a word. Then

Austerley felt brave enough to venture an excuse.

"The copy of the runes was six thousand years old. It had crumbled to pieces. It was perfectly understandable that the computer's reassembling software misaligned one of the runes. It was a freakish anomaly. Just one of those little upsets that every explorer experiences."

Kirkgordon stood to speak but no words came out. He stared at Austerley as if trying to detect the joke but none was forthcoming. Austerley was completely genuine in his belief that what had happened in that grave was just an unfortunate mishap.

"Just to clarify," Kirkgordon said, in a unwavering but extremely quiet voice which seemed intended to let the dead lie, "having the flesh ripped off my back by things I cannot even begin to describe, feeling my very core being sucked out of me, having Warren's long-dead yet fresh corpse slammed in my face, seeing the wildest and vilest sights, which still come to me every night in my 'mares, losing my family, losing the woman who stood by me when I went through the normal hells of this world, the woman who struggled to find my soul after that darkest day and who, when she did, recoiled from the horror that dwelt within me, nine months of isolation in that monastery finding what good remained in this world, this… this!… was a little upset? Dammit, Austerley, they ought to put you down for your own good."

Austerley coughed quietly.

"Churchy... thank you for getting me out." With

that, Austerley turned his own head to the window and the view outside. Kirkgordon stared at the chastised "lunatic" before him and fought to suppress the pity he felt for this troubled man.

"You're welcome, Indy," he murmured under his breath.

The rest of the flight consisted of a silence born from the hollow left by Austerley's apology. Kirkgordon tried to get some sleep but he felt the sharp talons again on his back. In his dreams he saw a large winged creature, as black as his mood had been in the monastery. It would fade in and out of clarity but he could always sense the immenseness of the creature. Next, his mind would be violated by Warren's half-digested face slamming into him. It had only just been recognizable from the black and white photograph of Warren at Miskatonic University. They had warned him but he hadn't listened. No one would touch Austerley or even contemplate his work. But the money had been good for babysitting this eccentric yet daft professor. Kirkgordon's lack of understanding of the Eldars had lured him into a false sense of security about the professor.

Then it all drifted away into a spinning green cauldron, which unwound to reveal a picture of tropical warmth. A woman was holding a lizard. She was smiling, half at the creature and half at him, her new-found love. Part of him roared with hunger for the beauty before him. Her long, dark hair curving onto her shapely torso, hips he remembered holding in the throes of passion. He dreamt that he was holding her tight, tasting her neck, the saltiness of her sweat like honey in his mouth. Body reacting to and encouraging body, souls touching on that most ethereal of plains. And then it swooped! She was carried away by the winged creature, hanging from its talons like a redundant corpse. He fired at it, blasting until it was out of sight. All the time he heard Austerley screaming at the guns.

"Twenty minutes to landing. Get yourself together, old bean." Farthington smiled at the wakening Kirkgordon. "You're back on babysitting duty."

Kirkgordon yawned and stretched and looked at the greyish cloud outside the window. He should have been going through the plans for Russia. How would they remain incognito? How would they track down this lead? Would they intercept, or just stake out the individual to see what he wanted? Would this mysterious threshold place be on time? But all he could see was a mother, a lover and, above all, the other half of his soul.

Chapter 4

Exit Stage Right

Farthington had a plan. It seemed like a complete over-elaboration to Kirkgordon but Austerley was extremely excited by the prospect of so many black limousines arriving at the aircraft. Five in total would be arriving together and then driven off in various different directions to confuse "our Russian friends". It wasn't often that Austerley got to ride in such a palatial car and he was itching to go. Wrapped in a large winter parka, thick grey trousers and large black boots, Austerley was the closest in appearance to a typical Russian. Kirkgordon preferred to wear his trekking jacket with numerous tight tops underneath, but at least his black track bottoms and baseball boots gave him the look of an average Joe. Farthington remained in his crisp suit with white shirt and tie, over which was a large grey coat and an umbrella and bowler hat that completed the "civil service abroad" look.

"Trust no one," Farthington whispered to Kirkgordon on exiting the aircraft, handing him an automatic as they headed for the vehicles.

"I don't!" Kirkgordon retorted, promptly handing the weapon back. He never liked the idea of being armed unnecessarily. There was Austerley to think about. He'd start singing loony tunes if he caught a glimpse of the weapon. Also, the Federal Security Bureau were bound to be on their tail, otherwise, why bother with the limousines? Experience had taught Kirkgordon that it was often better to blend in than to stand out, better to talk your way out than to come out fighting.

Austerley clambered into the middle of the back seat of the limo. Spreading out his limbs and his girth, he was in a good mood. At last some adventure was coming his way and he could start re-investigating the Eldars. Better than that, this Farthington guy seemed to want to bankroll it all. Funny how life worked out. Still, it was good to have Kirkgordon about. He knew how to handle himself and, what with early indications of Zahn, there was likely to be some action. As his thoughts turned to finding the seeker of Zahn's music, Austerley was rudely pushed to the far edge of the seat by Kirkgordon. Farthington occupied the seat facing them and shortly afterwards the limo pulled away.

"Where to?" Farthington inquired. "I refrained from asking until now so that none of the other drivers would know." Although Farthington had been staring directly at Austerley, it was Kirkgordon who replied.

"Downtown. Central shopping area."

"Did our expert tell you this?" Farthington looked at Austerley before flicking his head in the direction of Kirkgordon. Austerley had a quizzical look on his face, but it lightened at Kirkgordon's reply.

"Just need a few things. Better to be prepared."

"We have an ample arsenal at your disposal if required."

"I specialize. So, much appreciated, but I prefer my own gear, if you don't mind," smiled the former bodyguard. "Once I get sorted then we can follow some of Austerley's ideas for tailing this fellow. Happy, old bean?"

"Absolutely, old chap, but do not be tardy, we have a lot of work to do." Farthington missed Austerley's momentary look of panic on hearing that he supposedly had "ideas".

Austerley stared out of the window at the passing buildings and minutiae of everyday life. Bus stops, cars, new apartments, closed factories, older women carrying groceries. Everything had a grimness to its face. He knew the looks in the eyes of the people, the dashed hopes in their souls. It was a pervasive feeling despite the major changes in recent decades. He felt it too. Some people took hope from the small things of life continuing, from friends and family climbing the ladders. Too many years studying the Eldars had blunted this defence for him. Now he was as forlorn as these citizens. He wallowed in the pitiful scene outside. A final few calm moments before the flood.

The door opening was a surprise, as the car was still travelling. It was slowing down, approaching some traffic lights, but still moving all the same and so the shock was palatable. Austerley had no time to react as he felt his collar pulled and he was half carried, half thrown from the car and smartly hauled down a nearby side street. Looking down he saw Kirkgordon's boots. Bugger! This meant trouble.

Farthington's shout of "Stop!" could be heard behind them but Kirkgordon continued with the extraction and increased his pace. In a half-crouched form, legs stumbling, being pulled as he was, Austerley didn't get any opportunity to raise his head. Instead, he saw pavements and road surfaces pass by. There were open doors and kitchen floors. Shouts went up, from residents he supposed, and the clatter of items falling from tables was heard in their wake. At first, he could hear Farthington's shouts. Then the voices became Russian, with cries of "down here" and "cut them off over there".

Austerley was out of breath and feeling physically sick but his guide was relentless. Gradually, he realized that the hue and cry was dissipating and Kirkgordon was slowing. Then came the darkness and the slamming of a metal door behind them. Nausea overcame Austerley and he threw up on the floor. He started to cough but felt a hand clasp his mouth with a quiet but sharp "shush".

Time spent in the dark is often hard to quantify but Austerley reckoned a good ten minutes passed before the hand released his mouth. Outside he had heard the world continue in its quiet way, a distinct jackhammer punctuating the relatively calm back street his hidey-hole was in. Once, a couple of girls giggled their way past, and he also heard a man with a gruff voice shout into a mobile phone insisting he was not "bloody well late". Austerley's command of Russian was good and he recognized the local accent of all these voices. Racing through his head were random ideas of why Kirkgordon might have taken such evasive action. Nothing untoward had happened. Clearly, Farthington had been shocked at the developments. Eventually the silence had lasted long enough for Austerley to venture a question.

"Wh..." He was cut off immediately by the hand going over his mouth again.

"Indy," Kirkgordon whispered, in a calm but clearly bothered tone as if in a state of alert, "did you tell Farthington anything about your history here in Russia? Does he know where you might be going?"

The hand didn't remove itself from his mouth so Austerley just shook his head gently. He felt Kirkgordon's breath on his neck, controlled but deep. Although the outside ambience was all that could be heard, the internal whirring of Kirkgordon's mind was all too evident.

Suddenly there was a slight click and the door of the hidey-hole was prised open slightly. A torch shone into the darkness but Austerley realized there were some boxes between himself and the new arrivals. The hand on his mouth had gone but he had heard no movement from Kirkgordon. Shining over his head was the light from the torch, onto what he realized was the back wall of a metal container. An authoritative Russian voice ordered the two British runaways to come out. Austerley swallowed hard. He knew the long history of Russia's secret police and he had no desire to see if it was still as effective. Despite flicking here and there across the back wall, it was clear that the circle of light from the torch was growing steadily. Quiet but deliberate footsteps confirmed Austerley's suspicions of the ever-increasing proximity of the owner of the voice.

"Ah, Mr Austerley, if you would be so kind as to step out from..." Thud!

Austerley gingerly stood up and peered over the boxes to see a prone man wearing a grey bomber jacket and black trousers with black boots. Then his eyes were drawn to the figure at the door beckoning him forward.

"Indy, move!" came the hushed but imperative call.

In his haste, Austerley's footsteps rang out inside the container. An exasperated "Flaming nora" introduced another neck grab and frogmarch.

Thankfully, five minutes later Kirkgordon concluded their escape and hastened them both into a shambolic roadside café.

"Get the coffees, then come over and sit down. I'll explain what's going on," Kirkgordon whispered. Austerley waited in the small queue before ordering. He had to adjust his accent once he had heard the lady behind the serving counter speak. They were not as far downtown as he had thought. Still, a coffee was welcome, if only to wash the sick taste out of his mouth.

Kirkgordon had found a table near the back of the café as far away from the stewed vegetable smells of the kitchen as possible. The room had one entrance from the street, one into the kitchen beside the serving hatch and one further one with nearby toilet facilities indicated on it. Having positioned himself at a table close to the toilets, Kirkgordon was surveying the street and kitchen doors. The café was about half-full, mainly of workmen with large coats and fluorescent tops covering boiler suits.

"Why did we have to run?" Austerley asked.

"We were being followed. They must have had a heck of a number of cars to follow five limos. But we are operating on the assumption of a threat to the world, to the planet or something like that. If we are coming to eliminate a danger, a danger to all, why didn't the Russians know we would be here? Why not cooperate with them? Time is important, so why are we working under their radar?"

"I don't think Farthington was being like that," postulated Austerley, "he was merely concentrating efforts. Not diluting them, giving them all to us."

"For someone who has seen such horrors, you have much too decent an opinion of others," Kirkgordon said, shaking his head. "No, he wants something for himself, or his bosses. What's so potent about this music? Can it control something, or entice it? What's the power angle? It can't be money."

"But Farthington is government. British government. It said so on his card. The government's not going to go around capturing occultic music."

"Exactly. It's not. How do you know he's really government, by the way? Do you trust his card?" Kirkgordon sniffed offence at Austerley.

"But the Americans were with him."

"And they were who, exactly? And where's our diplomatic immunity? The guy I dropped was FSB. Carried the card."

"Federal Security Bureau? You killed an FSB man? Hell!" Austerley was shaking now.

"As if! He's just going to have a very sore head." Kirkgordon stared intently at his coffee. "Do you still have contacts here? From the darker elements, I mean."

"...Why?" The question was dragged out slowly and reluctantly from his mouth. He didn't want to see these particular dark elements again.

"We need to cut out the others for the moment, until we get a grasp on what's what. If this street is appearing then the darker elements will know. I doubt the FSB or Farthington will have those contacts. We need to go to them."

"They nearly killed me last time, you know that?"

"Yeah, but there's no other way to do this." Looking at Austerley, Kirkgordon wondered whether the returnee would be up to the task. Dammit, it was hardly a choice – he'd have to be up to it. "Oh and, Indy, one more thing. Do you know where we are, cos I haven't a baldies!"

Chapter 5

Meeting an Old Friend

It was now sometime after midnight and Kirkgordon felt as lost as he had back in the café. Austerley had taken him on a wild goose chase around Moscow, first finding out exactly where they were and then tracking down some old contacts. Most of Austerley's previous acquaintances had supposedly been rounded up by the "authorities". This seemed questionable, as the methods for rounding these people up seemed too sloppy for the FSB. Indeed, there had been a few deaths that had been seen in public.

How had it got to this? thought Kirkgordon. The

night chill made his breath appear in front of him in white condensation and he was thankful for the woollen hat perched on his head which he had stolen from a market stall. Well, not really stolen, as he had lobbed a few notes onto the stall table out of the view of the purveyor. Keeping hidden was paramount at this time. Thankfully, for all his hamfistedness, Austerley blended in perfectly with this culture. Morose and wrapped up like a duvet convention, he even had that depressive amble. Dammit, he was made for here.

They were crouched behind some cardboard boxes, waiting in the gloom of an alleyway for one of Austerley's contacts. Despite having interrogated the former asylum inmate about this contact, all Kirkgordon had got out of him was that he would know who the contact was when he met him.

It was now six hours since they had last seen any FSB and neither had there been further pursuit from Farthington. And yet, there was more of an edge now to Austerley. He would rock nervously side to side as he waited, chewing on his lip despite the cold air. The large gloves he was wearing didn't disguise that he was counting his fingers through them. What was making Indy so edgy? The condensation spat out from Kirkgordon's mouth as he inadvertently whispered a solemn prayer. His senses were screaming something at him. There was the smell of decay, of bodily corruption, in the air. The hairs on his arms rose as one. Then came the tap of a cane on the cobbled alley surface.

The figure groped along the shadows of the

alleyway, leaning heavily on its aid. Kirkgordon could have sworn Austerley was positively shaking as the figure came closer. As it reached them, it blended into the shadows and it was impossible to make out any distinction beyond the fact it that was vaguely a biped. The figure spoke a few guttural utterances to Austerley which Kirkgordon struggled to understand. A wave of a presumed hand left the bodyguard believing that the reason for his accompanying Austerley was being debated, but he could make out little else. Despite his obvious discomfort, Austerley was soon peppering the shadow figure with questions regarding Zahn's music. The grunted half-sounds that returned were clearly being understood, as Austerley consistently pushed for deeper answers.

It was less than five minutes before the unknown figure was tapping a retreat back down the alley, the cane once again clipping its way in a choppy rhythm. Austerley stood and watched until it had disappeared.

"Well?" asked Kirkgordon, "Did you get what we need?"

"He created some of the most magnificent, if distasteful, of images. I acquired one in Paris once, from a very small back-street dealership. The fool never knew the real value of it." Austerley pondered deeply. "It was astonishing how lifelike he made the damn things. But then I guess he didn't need an imagination." Closing his eyes, Austerley drifted to a place far away, to a framed work of art he had once held in his hands. Yes, it was damned good.

"What on earth are you on about?" interrupted Kirkgordon, stabbing a finger into Austerley's side to wake him from his reminiscences.

"Pickman," sniffed the heavily wrapped asylum dischargee. "Richard Upton Pickman, *artiste terrible*! He painted things that most on this earth never get to see, or certainly only see once."

"And that was him... this Pickman fellow?"

"Yes... well, no... not exactly."

"You're scaring me, Indy. What do you mean, not exactly?"

"Well... I've never seen one before... a ghoul, I mean. You hear and you see pictures. In fact, the painting I have is a ghoul by Pickman, but I swear they are worse up close. I'm glad he stayed in the dark."

"So who was that? Was it Pickman?" Kirkgordon was frustrated at being unable to enter the loop of Austerley's mind.

"You're right. Who *was* that is exactly the point. That, my friend, used to be Pickman."

"Hey, hang on," said Kirkgordon, his mind feeling that it had just missed the train, "used to be?"

"Yes, used to be. He's just a ghoul now. He doesn't even remember his paintings. It's quite sad. Are you okay?"

"No," Kirkgordon openly admitted. "Let's go before I start to process this... that was just a contact... okay Indy, just a contact."

"Okay," Austerley whispered. "Just a very old and dead one!"

"Austerley!"
"What?"
"Just shut it!"

The occasional distant car could be heard from the nearby road, its diesel engine thumping into the night. Otherwise, the only sound was the steady swish and swash of the river up against the banks. The recent cold spell had left the river at a lowish ebb and it was more lapping than flowing against the embankment edges. A stillness was in the air, due to the common sense of all but two creatures to get inside and remain there until sunrise. Sat under a bridge, one of the creatures was trying very hard to focus on certain material facts and not to drift into pondering where certain encounters had come from or were going to. The other creature had drifted into these worlds in his mind many moons ago and positively enjoyed his musings, if not the acquaintances that one met during these explorations.

"Okay, Indy. All things considered, what have we got to go on?" Kirkgordon was forcibly calm, easing each word out in a perfect rhythm, showing he was in control. But he was having to work damn hard at it.

"Well, I reckon, and you'll have to trust me on this, but the thing is... you see, it must be hard when the change comes... I mean voice boxes and that... they just don't talk like we do and the memory must go with lack of practice... I think he did rather well."

"Indy," hissed Kirkgordon, "I don't care about him... it... whatever it was. What do we know? Just tell me what we know now that we didn't know before we met him... it... that."

"They say Carter met him once."

"Shut it! Right now! We don't do Carter! Never. Understand? Dammit, Austerley. God forgive me, but there are times I wish you'd been left to rot in that graveyard. Or that loony house. Just tell me what he or it or whatever that blasted thing was said! No more, no less. Got it?" Kirkgordon was an inch from Austerley's with a coiled torrent of anger on his face. Austerley gulped.

"Sure. Okay. Whatever. No Carter. Got it. Well, let me see. I've got an address and a time. Well, more of a window, really."

"Where and when?"

"About an hour's time."

"What? Didn't you think it was kinda important to tell me that straight away? We need to move! Where?"

"It's a side street beside a restaurant not far from here. Although it's only in the early hours that the place will be open, it always was. Used to get a really good vodka in there. Yes, it was an exquisite place to be back then, lots of culture, people to see that you just never got to meet on the outside. Big open fire, too. I wonder if the seat that she put there is still there."

"Great, so it'll be there in an hour. Time to get off your arse then, Indy. We got some music to grab. Can we see the alley from the restaurant?"

"Should be able to, provided it hasn't changed." Austerley was drifting to a happier time and the seeping of a faint smile crossed his visage. "It can't have changed... maybe she's there. Vodka neat."

"Up now," interrupted Kirkgordon, "and get with it. If it's an old haunt, the FSB might be about too, maybe even Farthington."

"All right, Churchy, let's go. I need my bloody bed, mind!" They trudged back up to the street from under the bridge. All was quiet, and Kirkgordon started to map out how getting into the soon-to-emerge street was going to go down. Then a thought struck him.

"Who the hell's 'she'?"

Chapter 6

Table for Two

Anyone watching the occupants of the table by the window in that rather strange restaurant would be forgiven for thinking the two occupants were not part of the same party. One individual sat smiling, casually glancing around at the few people sat at dimly lit tables in shadowy corners. Occasionally he would nod to one or two people, raising his small glass of vodka just a touch to say cheers. For him, the world was at peace. As for the other gentleman, there seemed to be a distinct edge to his demeanour. Despite trying to present an easy appearance, his constant glances out of the nearby window and furtive stares at the room's other occupants betrayed a distrust of his whole surroundings. His vodka glass had yet to achieve airborne status.

"It really hasn't changed much at all," beamed Austerley. "The drapes still look magnificent, the floor is still showing that fantastic wooden sheen and the clientele, well, still nefariously wonderful!" The plush purple drapes showed little signs of age; neither did the lacquer on the floor. But the clientele were distinctly not to Kirkgordon's liking.

"Do you know any of them? Are they all normal? I mean normal for here, this place, I mean..."

"Freaks," Austerley interjected. "Asylum freaks, ne'er-do-wells, weirdos? Is that your inference?" He sneered the question down the barrels of his nostrils.

"Yeah!" Kirkgordon replied, "Mental cases, like you. Bloody dabblers."

Taking the offence on the chin, Austerley surveyed again his surroundings. Smiling wildly and raising his glass on several occasions, he assessed everything before turning back to Kirkgordon.

"Nearly all freaks, my friend."

"Nearly?"

"Your two o'clock, back wall. Not a freak. Not even a mental case."

"Got him. Anyone else?"

"Behind you, sipping tea, eating goulash. Definitely not from here."

"Here weirdo land or here Russia?"

"Here Russia."

"Any others?"

"Your four o'clock, gentleman with the beard and rough-looking clothes."

"Yes, but with strangely snug-looking footwear, black and stylish. I guess Farthington didn't get much notice either about the street's appearance. Don't look!"

It was too late; Farthington was already nodding an acknowledgement to Austerley.

"How the blazes did he spot us?" Austerley asked.

"He knew the area to look in. Possibly not precisely, but definitely the area. That's why he was so bothered when we headed downtown. And I don't think he knew the time."

Kirkgordon's distrust of Farthington was beginning to rub off on Austerley and a little bit of panic was pushing steadily into the Elder expert's mind. The walls seemed to loom in somewhat and the dining area that had been reminding him of such pleasant, if weird, times of yesteryear began to resemble the room where he had had his meals at the asylum. Sure, you could eat and drink without interruption, but if you got up to leave before time... well, nowhere else had he ever been bludgeoned into a seat.

Just as the darkness seemed to destroy the once-grand vista before him, another vision leapt before his eyes, like a phoenix rising. She was a bird of another variety, possibly of his own species but one could never really tell in this place, and her plumage was magnificent. Austerley's ruddy complexion burst into a glorious red as a familiar accent rang in his ears.

"Darling, oh darling, how very long you have been away. And time has been hard, I see. You have been gone too long, too long without the attention of your friends. Let me look at you, you handsome brute! Older yes, but fabulous, just fabulous. You could almost be from the old country. Seven hundred years I waited before seeing a vision like you and then you ran off. Oh, but now you're back. The Highland Count returns."

Kirkgordon was quite aghast at this intrusion into the sinister tableau. It was like a circus clown had rampaged across the stabbing scene in Shakespeare's *Julius Caesar*. No, clown was not right, this was a *tour de force*, this was a woman who could steal any show or take over any curtain call. Some six foot tall, she was curvaceous but trim. Everything about her screamed of a fulsome and fiery landlady, save one definitive exception. Her complexion was extremely white, like she was from the Arctic Circle. This contrasted with her jet-black hair, long and bouncy, which cascaded over her ample shoulders to frame an impressive cleavage. Attired in a tight, shiny black dress complete with wide collar, she looked like a Halloween partygoer with an exceptional figure. As Kirkgordon noted, Austerley was certainly captivated.

"How have you been, my Fire, my Passion, my lover? You have changed somewhat, that I can see, and you were afraid just now, but I see Calandra has ignited your soul once again. Stoked up your loins and filled your mind with dreams of wild and passionate embraces on moonlit nights. Am I right, my essence?" Kirkgordon nearly choked as "Calandra", with one hand, spun Austerley's seat round so that he faced her and then proceeded to straddle him, revealing two milk-white, long, slender legs through the slits in her skirt. Austerley's eyes started to water as the tableau-breaker sat facing him on his lap, presenting her pale but copious chest before his eyes. Kirkgordon couldn't help himself. He folded double with laughter.

"And who is your amused little friend? Let me look at him as he has been looking at everyone else here tonight. Well, darling, once again you choose so well your friends. Mature, like yourself, but the frame I like! Oh yes. But those eyes... they have seen the darkness. The evil, yes, but also the pain of losing a lover, *n'est pas*? Oh darling, be gentle with him for he is very fragile."

It was like being psychoanalysed by Greta Garbo. Kirkgordon was amused, stunned and touched all at once. Despite every sense in his body screaming "vampire", he found himself being seduced by this purported creature of the night, at least on a maternal level. Austerley, however, had clearly been well past the maternal level!

Calandra turned again to Austerley and began to whisper in his ear. If it had been possible, Indy would have blushed even deeper but his cheeks could not support any further reddening. Again a slight smile crossed Kirkgordon's lips, but now his mind was racing. Farthington sat with just a drink, watching the room. The man sat at their two o'clock. Russian. Again just a drink. Watching. The room was laced with several of Calandra's horde. And one other. One other that just wasn't fitting. Foreign but not strange. Foreign but not Elder. Foreign but not spooked by the company. Why choose here? Why eat here late at night? Farthington had a reason. The Russian was probably FSB, tailing Farthington. Or maybe even themselves. But this foreigner had just been sitting eating his goulash and was now calmly consuming a small dessert.

"Calandra?" said Kirkgordon.

"Yes, darling?"

"Can I steal you from that rugged beast of yours?"

"Only for a word, darling. If you mean to ravage me, you'll have to fight a duel. But I warn you, this stallion won last time."

It felt like being in a really poor B-movie. The dialogue tripped off her tongue with the alacrity of a gazelle, but her sincerity cut him cold to the core as he realized she wasn't joking. What on earth was Indy's past life like? pondered Kirkgordon. Part of his brain held up a large placard saying: We don't want to know! A leg whipped across his lap and that heaving cleavage brought him abruptly back to his purpose.

"The man across from us, Calandra. Tell me, do

you know him? Has he been in here before?"

The voluptuous temptress glanced quickly before running a hand around the back of Kirkgordon's neck. She drew close to him, gently breathing into his ear, and whispered a quiet "No, and no." Her breath and the touch of her hand were both as icy as Kirkgordon had ever felt. Calandra broke off and scanned the man sat across. She began to turn back to Kirkgordon but then sharply checked her eyes back on to the man. When she looked again at Kirkgordon her eyes were vacant for her mind was elsewhere, wandering through time and space searching for what she had just seen. After a minute she seemed to arrive at a place and she smiled lusciously, even licking her lips just a touch.

"Well, well. I know those eyes. Not the face, never seen the face, but those eyes. I remember the music. He was such a player. The rise and fall of the bow, the exhilaration in your soul, the places he touched. Oh, and when he played the other music... I see it all again in his eyes. Every last detail. Every note and grace note. Every tone that no one else could produce. It is Zahn. Stake me down, but it's Zahn." Her face was lost in wonder such as Kirkgordon had never seen. It was almost like she was experiencing a sexual high, so involved was her body in the memory.

"Are you telling me that's Zahn? He's been dead for years. How is he here?"

"No, darling. You young thing, you. Not Zahn himself. Zahn's eyes. That is a descendant of Zahn."

Kirkgordon nearly asked if she was sure but the ecstasy across her face was confirmation enough. He thought long and hard, trying to piece the puzzle together. Why? Why is he here? Why do the FSB want to be in on this? Who is Farthington, really? And why does he need our help? Calandra's cold touch on his cheek brought Kirkgordon back to his senses.

"Darling, he's leaving."

Oh hell, thought Kirkgordon. In all the drama of Calandra's arrival he hadn't noticed the passing of time. It was going down now and Zahn's offspring was clearly in on it.

"Calandra, it's about to get messy. Myself and Indy here," he pointed at Austerley, "are going to get up and leave and at least two men will try to stop us. They are both likely to be quite proficient in using their fists or some concealed weapons on their persons. I apologize if I break anything in preventing them from impeding us."

"Darling, they won't stop you. Leave it to Calandra. After seven hundred years I know how to handle men."

Kirkgordon couldn't stop himself asking.

"Are you a vampire?"

"You little child," laughed Calandra aloud, "I am so much more!" A vision of black clothing and white flesh shrieked across the room. She unfolded wings with an enormous span, and Kirkgordon saw Farthington and the supposed FSB man fall back from their seats beneath the aged wonder.

"She did that, but without the gown, when we..."

Austerley's brief reminiscence was curtailed by an all-too-familiar hand grabbing him by the collar and hauling him out of the restaurant. Struggling for breath, Austerley could hear the screams of two men meeting the darker side of his former lover. And then he heard one very pointed comment in his right ear.

"Never, ever, tell me about your sex life with that woman!"

Chapter 7

Street Knowledge

Zahn's descendant was calmly walking down the alley adjacent to the restaurant. He had clearly not heard the shrieks from inside, or he had chosen to ignore them. The foreigner was a little over five foot six inches with thick black hair and a wiry figure which seemed to waddle as it strolled down the side street, hips rising and falling like he was on a catwalk. At least he's not too big to handle, thought Kirkgordon, but then he dismissed that thought as he remembered Calandra's attack on Farthington and the FSB man. Clearly this shadowy world he was operating in was not one to be trifled with or estimated in normal proportions.

Austerley was recovering alongside. Part of him, mainly his body, was tired of this charging about and constant commotion. It was also regretting leaving his old lover for this rather different scenario. The other part of him, the part that had first found his lover and all the other weird and wonderful things in his life, was bursting to rise to the surface. Like a school kid at the sweet stall, his lips were salivating. Only the lack of breath stopped his body from fully embracing his wonderment.

Kirkgordon, holding himself and Austerley against the shadows, watched closely as Zahn junior continued along the alley. Another few steps, he thought, and they could continue a little further while keeping far enough away to not attract attention. Kirkgordon blinked. The foreigner was gone. Kirkgordon scanned the surroundings, desperately hoping to see some sign of the man. Nothing. Austerley was dumbstruck and could offer no help. Dammit. There was no other option.

Hauling Austerley to his feet, Kirkgordon swiftly, but with eyes systematically scanning the alley, raced down to the spot where the man had disappeared. On reaching it he probed the floor, searching for some sort of false pavement or covered hole. Then he raced to the walls at the side, seeking crevices. Nothing, just nothing. Blast it. There had to be some sort of passage into this street. Methodically, one brick at a time, he worked the wall, pushing and jabbing at the obstruction, but nothing gave. Out of the corner of his eye he could

Crescendo!

see Austerley just standing there, looking straight ahead, beyond where the foreigner had disappeared.

"Indy, stop standing around, you lazy swine, and help me check these walls." He had covered all of the wall now and was rechecking desperately. Nothing at all. Not even a hint of something giving way. And, dammit, look at him!

"Austerley, come on." But Austerley continued in his forward stare, totally motionless. He didn't flinch until his heavy eyelids suddenly flicked up with a lightness that spoke of inspiration. Austerley walked forward calmly and slowly and then... vanished.

Kirkgordon's mind was racing. He realized the solution to the foreigner's disappearance was now before him even though he didn't understand it. He swore at Austerley for being so damn foolish as to just charge on ahead. But the survivalist part of him was registering awareness of the cries of people exiting a restaurant just around the corner. By the sounds of it, they hadn't enjoyed their meal. Kirkgordon never liked the unknown, never relished going into a situation blind, and now he was not only about to do that but he was going to vanish into a place that moved around and was clearly not of this world. Bugger!

Farthington came racing round the corner, blood pouring from beside his right ear. He paid no attention to the deep gouge that had been ripped into his skin, instead scanning the alley ahead of him. He stopped dead in his tracks, squinting into the alley, disbelieving what he saw. Or rather the lack of what he saw. Nothing had changed from his earlier scouting. From the far end of the alley he saw a man dressed in a heavy blue parka jacket walk towards him accompanied by a large Alsatian dog. The man eyed him suspiciously as he strolled by with the dog. Farthington didn't mind the look that asked what he was doing here, but he noticed that the man never looked back up the alley. After grunting an under-the-breath rebuke at himself, Farthington exited the area. He knew the FSB man could not be far behind.

Presently, an FSB man did come round that corner. Like Farthington, he scanned the alley, and wandered round a little before calling his backup to pick him up. A minute later he drove off in a service car. And the alley fell silent.

But someone else was watching. After a minute's silence she stepped out from the shadows, her pale face undeterred by the cold of a Moscow night. Her heels clipped as she strode up the alley and the tight black leather outfit squeaked occasionally as her curvaceous figure eased along. She looked around, surveying the alley. Then she looked dead ahead and strode straight through the vanishing point.

Kirkgordon's senses were on edge and his comfort zone was last seen checking onto a fast jet going in the opposite direction. Focus man, dammit, focus. Where is Indy? Where's the stupid clown gone now? Then it struck Kirkgordon: was he still in the same alley? The walls looked like a continuation, a perfect join, but they were not a match to the outlook he had had just a moment ago. The alley had previously had only another two hundred yards to run and yet now he could see another five hundred yards of alley. Also, the buildings were getting taller for the remainder of the alley whereas before they had been getting smaller. Without making a sound, he glided to the end of the alley and was confronted by a sign. Улица на пороге. So he was here. Right place, right time. But where was Austerley?

He heard a faint noise. A door closing. Soundlessly, Kirkgordon rounded the corner to enter the street fully and was amazed to see how narrow and tall it was. Still in the same style as the area of Moscow they were in... or had been in. The street was getting steeper and some of the buildings seemed to overhang and nearly touch each other. Part of him was shaking now, down in his core, and he struggled to control it. He listened carefully. Further up on the left. That noise again. A door closing for the second time. Kirkgordon sprinted up the street, defying the slope.

Racing up the hill, Kirkgordon was aware of the end of this street approaching. There was a wall that loomed over, looking down the street. As he got closer to this goal he slowed his pace, looking for the elusive door he had twice heard closing. Where was it? His mind focused on trying to remember the direction, the level of the noise, had it echoed? No. There was nothing definitive that could guide him further. He would have to search each house one by one. Blast! Then he heard the shrieks.

They were definitely shrieks, that is, more than one source. One was that of a frightened man, wild and unashamed, terror screaming from every pore. But there were also shrieks of wild things, beasts of some sort. Despite the echoing along the street, he was able to distinguish the sound as coming from the third house from the end on his left-hand side. He raced up to the front door only to find it locked. Without hesitating, Kirkgordon kicked viciously at the handle, knocking the knob off before smashing the flimsy lock apart with the sole of his foot. The shrieks continued, coming from higher floors. Vaulting two stairs at a time, Kirkgordon drove himself up at pace until he reached the top floor. Catching his breath momentarily, he surveyed the area and saw a door at the far end of the landing. The door was bulging like it was about to explode, and loud bangs and thumps could be heard from beyond it. The shrieks were definitely coming from inside.

"Arghhhhhh! No! Of all that's holy, noooooooo!"

That was Austerley's voice. Kirkgordon reacted by racing at the door and hitting it with all the might of his right shoulder. The door was taken clean off its hinges and continued, along with Kirkgordon, until they both hit the opposite wall. Pain racked his shoulder as he crumpled to the ground but, as he rolled briefly on the floor, his scan of the room was already assimilating everything. A creature stood in the middle of the room, holding in one hand some sheet music and in the other, Austerley, by the throat. The horror of a creature's face having no eyes or mouth makes quite an impact on your mind. Two small horns adorned a head that seemed almost human, but minus the redeeming facial features. Its skin was like beaten black leather and its ears were pointed. It had two large wings folded across its back and four fingers with cruel barbed nails that held Austerley tight. A tail with a sharp-looking point was waving out behind the beast and it stood on two feet, each with four sharp talons. A surge of dread welled up inside Kirkgordon; he knew of only one way to deal with it.

The creature was so caught up in its prize that it ignored Kirkgordon until he broke an occasional table off its back. The force of the blow caused it to drop Austerley, who fell like a sack of potatoes to the floor, and the creature turned on Kirkgordon, extending its talon-tipped wings and moving into a semi-crouch. The crouch lasted all of a second. The creature sprung at Kirkgordon, who flung himself backward but failed to evade the flailing talons. His sides screamed as the points drove deep into his skin; he grunted, trying to suppress the surprise and panic inside. Years of training drove him back to his feet and forced his mind to think, and think fast.

Austerley was breathing but Kirkgordon doubted his awareness of the situation given that he was barely moving on the floor. The creature started to crouch again, still holding the sheet music in its hand, but then another figure in the distant corner of the room caught Kirkgordon's eye. In that glance, he recognized the foreigner, cowering. Further details would have to wait as the creature pounced. This time Kirkgordon was ready and had grabbed a broken piece of table off the floor. As the creature dropped down onto him, he drove this makeshift stake up at its throat, allowing the creature's considerable weight to force the impalement. With one hand extended and the target met, Kirkgordon had turned his back to the creature, a mistake punished by a ripping from its talons. It did not die immediately and continued to thrash at Kirkgordon's rear, causing him multiple extra lacerations. Eventually, the creature succumbed and Kirkgordon was able to half roll, half slither out from under the carcass. His torso was on fire from the pain but his training enabled him to pick himself up and assess the situation.

Austerley was prone on the floor and some blood could be seen seeping from his neck. Weakness was starting to overcome Kirkgordon's body and he was worried he would be unable to carry his partner from the building. The foreigner was still tucked up tight in the corner, shaking. The music manuscript was lying on the floor beside the creature's corpse, and Kirkgordon grabbed it, stuffing it inside his top. His head was starting to spin when he heard the voice.

"You... you ha... you have to destroy it. Now. Burn it, don't rip it up, just burn it... they need it... they won't stop... not 'til they have it." It was the foreigner. His voice was cracking, the fear in his eyes blazed for all to see, and yet Kirkgordon sensed an earnestness grounded in some sort of rationale.

"Why? Who wants it? What does it do?" Kirkgordon's eyes were starting to blur and he felt unsteady on his feet. The blood loss from his wounds was beginning to tell.

"The music will call him. My forefather was meant to do it but he was interrupted. So they killed him. And now I have the hands to play. They came in my dreams. Haunted me. Led me to this place. But I had the truth of it. He left letters to the family. So I came to destroy it. It must not be used. Burn it! Now, I implore you. For the sake of all humanity, burn it!"

He was half weeping, half shouting these instructions. Despite this noise, Kirkgordon could hear a faint beating in the background. Faint, but slowly increasing. A beating... no, a flapping, like wings. But not one wing. Many. Oh, hell!

They burst through the windows, the glass exploding into the room, causing shards to rip across Kirkgordon's face and body. If he had turned his back to avoid them he would have been unable to block the talons trying to rip out his throat. Instead, he managed to get a shielding arm up and was merely knocked off his feet into the wall. He tried to react as his training dictated but failed, only managing to raise his head so that he could see his enemy. The picture he saw invoked a terror which tore into his soul.

At least ten creatures similar to the one he had killed were now in the room. One was searching for something, ripping the clothes off Zahn's descendant in a wild search. This took a matter of seconds before the creature picked the foreigner up and tossed him out of the window. Kirkgordon assumed the man was already dead as he heard no scream on the descent, just a sickening thud as the fall was broken by the street below.

The other creatures were securing the room, one standing over Austerley and several coming to encircle Kirkgordon. The searcher now turned his attention to Austerley and quickly rifled through his victim's garb in a clumsy fashion. Watching, Kirkgordon tried to rise up to defend his partner but all his strength was gone. As the search would prove fruitless, he feared the worst for Indy but was mentally poleaxed when one of the other creatures picked up Austerley and flew out of the room with him. If he had had any energy left, Kirkgordon would have panicked as the searcher now turned to him. Instead, a sense of finality and dread overcame him and he prepared for the end. He felt the first rough searchings of the creature but then something quite unexpected happened.

A black shadow erupted into the room. Visually it was difficult to comprehend as there was so little contrast between it and the creatures. What Kirkgordon's brain could discern was the thudding of creature parts hitting the floor, the howls of pain and panic from these beasts and something else so sublime that his deteriorated senses nearly missed it. It was the smell of someone perspiring. Female, he thought, someone he recognized. As the last moments of consciousness were about to leave him, he thought to himself: Who is she? What is she? And thank you God, she's here!

Chapter 8

Chilled Flesh

Sunlight glimmered off the slightly rippling surface of the water, providing a backdrop of sublime beauty eclipsed only by the young family rolling around in friendly play on the nearest bank. A small toddler was lifting his top up and exposing his bare belly, causing ruptures of laughter from the baby lying on its back. The nineteen-seventies hairstyle, long and draped over the ears, so like the rock stars of that age, gave a cuteness to the toddler surpassed only by his beaming smile. The baby girl was delicate and yet also so secure, lying before her doting mother. The mother lifted her head and Kirkgordon stared into a memory all too distant.

The woman swung her auburn hair from one shoulder to the other, her green eyes fixed on Kirkgordon, and smiled briefly before allowing her tongue to run the length of her bottom lip. He knew that tell; Alana always did it when she was happy. No, not happy, more... contented, at peace, or was it joy? Whatever, she was always in the best of places when she did it. And the best of places had always involved Kirkgordon and their children. It had been so long since she'd run the length of her lip.

The children continued to laugh and giggle at each other, occasionally finding those noises new to their voices which caused such amusement. Alana kept a watchful eye but was constantly drawn back to Kirkgordon, penetrating his soul through his dark eyes. He had always wondered how she had found something to like in there, something to treasure in the darkest times. Since the crypt incident, he had become wilder, his cries in the night causing her such pain. First ramblings in the night and then physically lashing out, an unconscious crusader who only ended up striking the one he loved.

When she had left – by mutual consent, a plan to save her physical pain – they had held each other so tightly that they had left light bruises, keepsakes on one another. They still spoke, but he could hear her anger at the darkness within him. Austerley's name was never mentioned, the white elephant she sought with her blunderbuss. Unlike himself, Alana didn't have that shared pain that allowed him the chance to bestow pity on Austerley.

Suddenly the scene changed and he was lying in a bed. It was massively wide and he felt swamped, but his eyes quickly focused on the woman exiting the shower alcove across the room. As she took her lone towel and dried herself, he lay back, remembering each curve that was now exposed. He felt the hunger rising, realizing that he had been too long adrift from this island of refuge. Having caught him looking, Alana turned round with her hands on her hips, a comical towel wrapped round her head, and mouthed a teasing "What?" Surveying her glory he knew the script called for him to grab her and drag her under the covers. That was what he had done out in Portugal. But it had been too long and this wasn't even real, so he enjoyed the view until consciousness came to claim him.

With consciousness came the pain. The gorges across his back screamed their anger, forcing him to roll slightly and often to lift them from the couch he was lying on. Occasionally they would stick and he knew welts would form, so deep were the valleys impressed. A more general hurt existed across his fuller frame but it was lingering somewhere in the scenery, masked by the sharp stabbings of the gorges.

"Hey, sunshine!" His head flicked left to see Calandra standing in a crop top and panties. Her long black hair was wet, from showering he guessed, and her impressive form was fighting to occupy his mind through his watery eyes. He sighed and rolled his head back into the couch.

"That was kinda disappointing. Cheers for that. You sure know how to make a girl feel good." She had said it quite jovially but the hurt in her voice clambered out at the edges.

"Sorry."

"Just not recovered, then."

"No, it's not that."

"Well, thanks once again. My goodness, what does it take with you? A nurse's outfit? Or fully nude? It's been a while, but if nude is what it takes to get you going, I don't mind."

"Please, no. Don't do that!"

"Come on. Kinda taking a hit on self-confidence here."

"Sorry. It's just... I have someone... or rather, had. Sorry. It's not your lack of beauty... it's your jammed-to-the-hilt jar-load of it that's the problem..." Kirkgordon's voice tailed off as he returned to thinking about Alana.

"Sorry. Didn't know. You want me to put something else on?"

"I'd like to say suit yourself but to be honest... probably a good idea. Though my eyes do say different."

"Now you are buttering me up. A runner-up prize!"

"Trust me, there's a part of me stirring that will make me do something stupid, so kindly put something else on. Oh, and thank you!"

"For the view?" She stood there, defying Kirkgordon who had turned to look at his saviour.

"No. For saving me."

"Pleasure. I'm sorry I can't help your deep pain. I hope *she* can!"

When Calandra returned, she had added an open tracksuit top and a short black skirt. The view hadn't changed much but the tension was gone. With the physical urgings reduced, Kirkgordon's brain kicked in with some obvious questions. What had happened to her accent? Where were her wings? What age was she?

"Bit slow on it. But you did take a fair battering. Hell, so did I. They aren't real, if that's what's bothering you."

"What are they then? Where did they go...? I mean, they were massive!" His curiosity was aroused now and, forgetting his own maxim that he unendingly denounced Austerley with, yes, he decided to "go there".

"A physical projection of the mind. It's a neat trick. Look!" Calandra turned her back to Kirkgordon and dropped the tracksuit top before pulling the crop top over her head. Her bare back showed several slash marks. Suddenly, two enormous wings appeared on her back and beat gently. Kirkgordon felt a cool breeze on his face. Calandra turned round and unashamedly walked towards the couch, wings still unfurled. Kirkgordon tried to focus hard on the wings and not the exposed white flesh until she sat down on the edge of the couch, facing away from him again. The wings vanished and her scarred back was just inches from Kirkgordon's face.

"Touch my back! Look, nothing sexual, just

touch my back!" Kirkgordon ran his hand across her back. The skin was so cold, like touching the ice on a frozen pond; it took a while until the real depth of the coldness could be felt.

"So cold. How?"

"I am seven hundred years old. And this coldness, this curse, keeps me like this. That's why I look twenty-five."

"Actually I reckoned mid-thirties."

"Your charm is devastating. Okay, you're right, thirty-six to be accurate."

"What curse?"

"She did it. She killed him and left me like this." For the first time Kirkgordon heard her voice start to crack, the confidence overtaken by a chilly reticence. She turned and looked straight at Kirkgordon. "Can you imagine what it's like to be in your prime yet appear as a freak to the men you attract? How they cower at my touch, or wet themselves when they feel my skin? They fear me, just fear me! There's no closeness, never."

"Except Austerley. He would love you for it. You're the very thing he seeks."

"Yes," Calandra whispered, but tears were coming through now too, "but it's still a thing with him. Loved for being extraordinary, not for being me. He gave me comfort, physical relief, but not a mutual embrace. I hold him dear for what he did for me and I do care deeply for him. But I am a pet to him. Not an equal."

"Don't judge him too quickly. He's too ready to follow his curiosities, but there's a real person with real cravings in there. I saw his face in the restaurant. You mean a lot to him."

Kirkgordon was holding her cheek and she cried hard, eventually leaning into his shoulder. When she sat back up, she saw he was crying too.

"What?" she inquired of him. "You don't seem an overly emotional person. What?"

"You..." He let her see him enjoying her as his eyes wandered up and down her body. "You are so beautiful. I'm sorry."

For the first time since her lover died she felt a true embrace with no intention other than to tell her she was comforted. "Cally. Call me Cally. It's what my brother called me. No one else does." She reached for her top and pulled it back on over her head. All the time she stared deep into Kirkgordon's eyes and noted that he stared right back, never once seeking to take in a last look at her flesh. "Sorry for the whole flesh thing." She bowed her head almost in apology. A hand raised her head up and Kirkgordon kissed her forehead.

"And you can call me Churchy. Only Austerley ever uses it. As for the flesh – I'm a man, it's not like it wasn't enjoyable. But I think there's more to you than a hot body."

"A cold one, actually!"

"Yeah. And you're better off without that accent."

Chapter 9

Old Time Girl

Kirkgordon slept for much of the remainder of the day. When he did wake, Cally brought him some coffee and a little bread with butter. She explained that the small flat they were in belonged to an acquaintance who had had to flee Russia in a hurry, leaving her the key. In actuality, it was more of a bedsit. One side of the rather dreary situation was taken up with a modest kitchenette consisting of a small oven and hob arrangement, a sink, a fridge and an outdated microwave. They were a mishmash of colours, functional rather than decorative. The other side of the room was taken up by the couch Kirkgordon was lying on and a rather petite chair.

Cally sat in this chair while Kirkgordon slept, staring at him for long periods of time. In deference to him she had put on a pair of black jeans and a grey sweatshirt. For some reason she found herself relaxing in front of him, dropping her usual pretence even when he was awake. She enjoyed their banter and found it hard to accept this man as just a friend. She had a fondness for him that didn't know where to sit itself.

Kirkgordon's concerns about Austerley surfaced early in their conversations. Cally explained that Austerley must have been taken to the other realms by the winged creatures, the Nightgaunts. Many times over the years she had encountered them but never in such numbers. Despite Kirkgordon's protestations about how strong the beasts were, she remained resolute that they were some of the calmer creatures from the "darker places". As for retrieving Austerley, Cally quickly dashed any optimism Kirkgordon may have had.

"I don't know my way around there... wherever *there* is? We would be on our own in very foreign territory. It's a no-brainer, Churchy!"

Kirkgordon felt a closeness when she used that name. He also saw the worry in her face for her ex-lover Austerley. However, there was some good news.

"We have what they want, Churchy. They will come for it at some point."

"The manuscript? What do they want with it?

They don't even have eyes."

"It's not the Nightgaunts that want it. I told you, they are small creatures. Big talons, yes, but still pawns. Someone put them up to this. Someone wants that music."

"And Austerley? They killed Zahn's offspring but they flew away with Austerley. Why?"

"How well do you know Austerley? No, don't answer. Not well enough or you wouldn't have asked. You probably think him mad talking about all this Elder stuff."

"Not mad, no. Daft to get involved, yes. Stupid enough to keep pushing. But not mad."

"No, he's not mad. I tell you, for seven hundred years I've been living with this darkness and yet Austerley knows more than me. He understands the rituals, the meaning of things. He grasps the lore and the fact. He holds the horror within himself. But he does hold it. Most people think he is... loony tunes, is that the expression now? Well he may be a bit loony tunes but with the knowledge he has, anyone else would be dead. And at their own hand. He's stronger than you realize. But yes, he's more curious than the cat."

"So what? They actually want him. For what he knows."

"Churchy, listen. The people who get involved with this darkness, these Elder beings, not all of them understand how to bring things about. Generally, they have to research and find things from the past. To them, Austerley is like a walking encyclopedia. Somebody wants to do something and my guess is Austerley knows how. God help us."

It was clear that Calandra was thinking back to previous battles, with an occasional touch to her sides and knees, a nod to injuries sustained. Her eyes might be staring at the bland emulsion on the wall but what they saw was pain and hurt from the past. She juddered back into awareness when Kirkgordon proposed a new idea.

"So, if they want this manuscript, why don't we just burn it, here and now?" Kirkgordon threw the document to the floor and reached for a match from the kitchenette. He struck it and let it fall, only for Calandra to catch it in her hand.

"No! You can't burn it!"

"Why ever not? Without it they are stuffed!"

"Feel the paper. Does it feel like any paper you have ever felt? No, thought not. It's not paper of this world. You burn that and, yes, you will see ashes. But the manuscript will reform itself elsewhere, probably in the other worlds. Right where they want it. Our keeping it is a problem for them. They need to find us."

"So, just to recap, we have a music tune which some otherworldly beings want to do who-knows-what with, but probably some very bad thing. They have kidnapped the only person who might know what this is and put him in a place we can't reach. And we can't stop them because we can't destroy the music. All we can do is hide it from them." And, thought Kirkgordon, I am sitting in a small flat in Russia with a seven-hundred-year-old woman with huge wings, having been flashed and propositioned by her, though not unpleasantly, only for her to unburden her sorrows on my shoulder. And I got out of the bodyguard business because it got too exciting?

"Cally, can they find us?"

"Yes, and they will. We can evade them for maybe a week tops but they will track us down, and not by conventional methods either."

"Can you contact them?"

Calandra thought long and hard.

"Yes. It will shorten the time for them to find us, though."

"Okay, the way I see it, we are already marked. There's no good 'out' here. So I propose we fight on our own terms. We need to meet them and they need to bring Austerley. We need to smash and grab!"

"They'll not bring Austerley. We haven't got anything to offer. They'll just wait until they find us. Easier and safer for them."

"Yes, except we know how to destroy the manuscript. Permanently. So they will have to come."

"And how do we do that?" Calandra asked.

"How should I know? Time for some misdirection. We need Austerley. He'll understand all this, he'll know what to do."

"You believe that?"

"Yes. Well, he'll have the pieces. And we've got to hope he can put them together. All other routes are dead ends. Agreed?"

"Agreed!"

"Okay, so you have to find a contact."

"Hmmmm. Okay, I think I know how to do this. But Churchy, you'll need to avert your eyes. I'm afraid the dark world doesn't know Calandra, bearer of the grey sweatshirt and low-cost jeans. Time to wear the uniform again."

Calandra popped out for about an hour and when she returned she was carrying a large black holdall over her shoulder. Smiling broadly at Kirkgordon, she clanked into the room, the bag's contents being metal in nature. It was obvious she was going to change and so he closed his eyes and successfully fought the desire to sneak a peek at the stunning form he had seen earlier. After a short period of rustling and the occasional 'ting' of metal colliding, he felt a cold hand touch his cheek.

Standing before him was a vision of royalty and power. From the pointed black boots to the silver shin guards, the mid-thigh chain mail to the skimpy breastplate, the gauntlets running up her forearms to the plumaged helmet from under which flowed her lavish black hair, and the cross-shield to the sharp gleaming short sword: all gleamed with promises of power and sensuality. Kirkgordon laughed, thinking he had wandered into a particularly good fancy dress shop.

"It has been six hundred years and they didn't laugh then. At least, they stopped when I neutered the first five who did."

"Sorry. Trust me, it looks great, but maybe a bit

over the top for modern Russia."

"Given the time that has passed since I last met my contact he'll need this to recognize me." She laughed, then grew serious. "And fear me."

"Do you need company?"

"No. He's a man so I'll turn on the sexual side. Well, at least he was a man."

"When are you leaving?"

"Five minutes. I just need to get the door."

Kirkgordon was confused but watched as Calandra drew some designs on the floor with a thick piece of chalk. She then spoke some words he couldn't even begin to pronounce. Suddenly the floor began to glow and then it erupted into a bright light. Kirkgordon had to avert his eyes but he heard her say "see you in ten!" The room went quiet and resumed its normal level of brightness.

Lying back, Kirkgordon tried to switch his mind off and remember his dream from the morning. Annoyingly, he had just got back into watching Alana leaving the shower when the room blazed bright again and he heard the word "Bingo!"

"Did it go all right?"

"Yes it did. Apart from the outfit. Seems everywhere's gone a bit more modern. Felt like a tart on parade."

Kirkgordon laughed.

"Still looks good though."

"So, what's next?"

"We wait. Here. And I get out of this armour. I don't remember it being this tight."

Chapter 10

Russian Country Life

It had taken a day to get there and, if he was honest with himself, it wasn't worth the view. Kirkgordon watched his breath smoke in the morning cold and was thankful for the large bomber jacket he had picked up at a small street stall before they left Moscow. Also helping were the scarf, the gloves and the rather thick socks inside the uncomfortable but practical wellies. But cold had never really bothered him. Well, not the weather variety. The snow painted the ground a perfect pure white, the like of which was usually only seen on postcards. This particular postcard, however, was ruined by the copious broken-down farm machinery that littered the landscape. Amongst a number of trees and covered hedges sat once-proud industrial cultivating giants, now silent and impotent. They were falling apart piece by piece, rust spreading like a disease throughout the body. Kirkgordon wondered how long he had before this madness started affecting him in the same way. Would he start to go like Austerley?

No, the cold didn't bother him, unlike the chill that Calandra exuded. For a woman to whom he felt so closely drawn, he was constantly taken aback by the icy sharpness of her touch. Her leather jacket flapped as she paced quickly back toward him after completing a short scouting mission. He watched the black T-shirt hug her ample curves and enjoyed the black jeans snug around her thighs. Dammit, he missed Alana.

The train journey out of Moscow was uneventful and they had hiked for about four hours through the night after the bus routes had run out. To him it looked like any agricultural landscape in rural Russia, but Calandra had said this was the place. So many weird places around us, thought Kirkgordon, and we pass them every day. Like the crypt. Oh, damn Austerley and his desires. Ostriches had it so good. He wished he too could live a life of ignorance. But now he had been introduced to all this, he knew the inner compunction to stand in the fight against the unholy would be too strong. Although he and God were on a bout of silence, he knew he hadn't jumped the fence. Yes, he addressed his ultimate master, you and me need a conversation about all this one day.

Calandra's contact had been good. Apparently, in the days when she still could warm you with her touch, he had been a count of an old order and he had caused her some disservice. Debts had been called from whatever creature he was now, and an arrangement had been arrived at with Austerley's kidnappers. Nothing had been said about who they were and they seemed to have bought the story about destroying the manuscript. Or, they may not have done, Kirkgordon mused. Either way, they wanted it, and Calandra and himself were saving them from searching. Only when the kidnappers arrived would they see if Austerley was with them and know whether the bluff had worked.

"Beside the orange digger, the one with the broken bucket." Calandra smiled as she whispered this detail. In some ways she was like Austerley. Already she was relishing the storm that was coming and she had talked animatedly about what new beast or creature she might see. The Nightgaunts had been more than enough for Kirkgordon, who was used to being able to weigh the odds. Usually they were at least fifty-fifty, or, better still, stacked in his favour. In this strange world he was wandering like a young child: ignorant, wide-eyed and slightly scared. The odds were not measurable when he didn't know what was in the pack. Calandra stowed the manuscript inside her jacket. It made sense as she was the stronger fighter. He hoped she was a damn good one. The

Nightgaunts moved so swiftly and their talons had cut serious gorges into him. He could still feel his wounds, despite whatever ointment Calandra had put on him. Still, the physical pain was one thing. The mental horror, the shaking that his brain was going through just from the mere presence of these things on this dear earth, was too much. Austerley, although he had nights of wild terror, had learnt to embrace these changes, learnt to form some sort of appreciation. Austerley's contact in the alley had provoked only disgust in Kirkgordon, but Austerley had been almost pleased to see the thing. He had wondered at its beauty, for pity's sake.

Calandra was another thing entirely. No, not thing, person. Kirkgordon was convinced she was a person, even though she didn't fit any particular category of person in his head. At least one could appreciate her beauty. Also, she had deep bonds of respect and trust with Austerley. But she was worried. Kirkgordon had seen this in stronger parties before – usually he was that party, so he knew the game well. She was overcompensating with positivity. Telling the lesser party that all would be okay, over and over. She was trying to appear insurmountable. He would need to watch her back.

"They'll come up from over there. See the tunnel reaching into the ground about three foot wide? There. That's where. How many, I can't say."

Kirkgordon watched as Calandra picked up the staff she had carried with her from the room they had hidden away in. A staff seemed little protection from these creatures that were coming.

"Are you proficient with that thing?" Calandra threw Kirkgordon a mean and dirty look. She twisted the centre of the staff and two blades emerged from either end. A strong push about three quarters of the way along the staff opened a secret compartment and some ten knives dropped into her free hand to be quickly secreted on her person.

"Stand behind me when they come. I'll draw them close and you can pick and hit on the run." She was doing it again. Overprotective. Kirkgordon reached into his pocket and felt the small knife he had taken from her armoury in the flat. Calandra had had some extensive weaponry but he was unable to use just about all of it. Why she had picked out this staff, even with its hidden extras, he just didn't know. The sound of a car arriving brought his thoughts to a close.

It was a black limousine, the type of which Kirkgordon recognized as that he had been driven in at the airport. It drove up to the field they were in, cruising across the hard ground. From the passenger side an older, balding man dressed in a black suit, its crispness contrasting with his decrepit appearance, got out. He looked like he was ill, skin peeling in places and eyes wide and sombre. Reaching the rear door of the vehicle, he opened it with surprising alacrity for one so old. A familiar face emerged.

"Ah, Kirkgordon. You are rather unusual for an employee. However, you do have the manuscript as requested and so I think the return of your colleague is a fair arrangement for your services. Also I am happy to present your fee on deliverance of the document. With an added bonus for your quick work." Farthington's smile had the slickness of caramel and was probably just as sickly too. "As for your present company, I will be happy to let bygones be bygones, despite the injury she caused to me." Calandra sneered.

"Show me Austerley, then we talk."

"No doubt your colleague has mentioned we have other friends at our disposal. A more pleasant candour would be appreciated. No need for this to turn out nasty."

"Austerley! Please." Kirkgordon was scanning everywhere but he could not find any extras except for the man from the car and presumably a driver. Maybe another one or two inside as well.

"Very well, Kirkgordon." Farthington turned back to the car, reopening the rear door. "Mr Austerley, please step out."

A shaking figure emerged and the face that looked up at Kirkgordon was indeed Austerley but not the same one that had left him in the room on that cursed street. He had scratch marks all over his face, some much deeper than others. Shoulders hunched, he walked, or rather stumbled, towards Kirkgordon.

"Mr Austerley has been most helpful. And now the manuscript."

"What the hell have you done to him?" raged Calandra. The staff in her hand was now spinning in front of her. Austerley had dropped to his knees, clearly exhausted. Calandra made a beeline for Farthington who was standing beside him. The staff twirled at a manic pace and gleamed white at its ends. Farthington just smiled as she approached, and Kirkgordon watched the hole Calandra had pointed out earlier turn black as a sudden explosion of winged creatures emerged from it.

"Calandra, Nightgaunts!" roared Kirkgordon, drawing the knife from his jacket. Kirkgordon counted six Nightgaunts emerging; one came directly toward him while the others raced at Calandra, forming a protective line in front of Farthington. Even in the light of the day, their total blackness was shocking and the absence of eyes and mouth positively unholy. Kirkgordon forced himself to concentrate on his sole attacker rather than watch the fate of his colleagues.

Last time the speed of the Nightgaunts had surprised him but now he was ready for their agility. Hopefully his guile would be enough to counteract it. Setting down from flight about five feet in front of him, the gaunt coiled, ready to pounce. Kirkgordon froze to the spot, eyes fixed on his foe, carefully watching the talons hanging from the black arms. The gaunt suddenly launched forward, swinging its right arm, which Kirkgordon narrowly avoided by rolling to his right before scrambling back up to his feet. Turning, the gaunt again coiled for a second pounce. This time as it leaped forward its left arm swung the deadly shredding talons. This time rolling to his left, Kirkgordon was unfortunate to receive a slight raking to his back. The pain was palpable but he regained his stance. Dammit, he thought, this will have to end soon. It stared with its inadequacy of eyes, a sensation that was deeply troubling the recesses of Kirkgordon's mind. It seems to be thinking, he thought. Good.

Coiling tight before releasing, this time the gaunt swung both arms as it leaped at him. Sensing the opportunity, Kirkgordon sprang straight into the gaunt, feeling its arms encompass him, but not before he managed to position his arms, and hence his knife, above the wrapping limbs. Struggling against the pressure imposed by the gaunt's arms and the pain of the talons yet again ripping through the jacket into his flesh, he grabbed its head with his left hand and sliced hard with his blade through its neck. They fell together in a heap and the arms constricted tighter for a brief moment before falling limp. His heart beat hard, his breath struggled and he raised his head to see how his friends were faring.

Extremely well was the answer. Calandra was standing in front of Austerley surrounded by three gaunt corpses and two others were prone on the ground, howling in agony. Looking closer, Kirkgordon could see she wasn't fully resting on her left leg, which had a serious gouge in it and was bleeding intently. She was smiling, however, and started to demand things of Farthington.

"Who's it for? Who's after the music? Your protection's gone, little man, time to start piping a tune if you don't want to be lying side by side with these faceless scum!"

Calandra was putting everything into this questioning and it worried Kirkgordon. She was too keen, too pushy. Surely there was no rush now that the Nightgaunts were disabled? Some slightly more subtle but effective methods came to mind but then he realized that Calandra was hurrying for a reason. That leg did not look good.

"Protection?" laughed Farthington. He threw his head back and gave a theatrical laugh which reverberated around the whole area. The voice did not seem entirely earthly. "You have no idea who I am, do you? Or indeed what I am? Now hand me that manuscript or you will find out. You will look into the face of a hell you cannot comprehend. Остерегайтесь дыхание дракона, Mr Austerley!" And the laughter became raucous.

Kirkgordon looked directly at Austerley and saw a face full of dread and panic. Normally, Indy took pronouncements with ease but this was different. Despite his state of abuse and fatigue, his body was finding new ways to tremble. As he caught Kirkgordon's eye, he just shook his head, eyes wide in disbelief.

"What, Indy, what did he say?"

"Go! ... We need... need to... go! Остерегайтесь дыхание дракона. Вот дерьмо!" Calandra seemed to be caught in a moment of panic, shaking where she stood. But she regrouped and started spinning her staff, which started glowing white at either end. At least someone's got a handle on what's happening, thought Kirkgordon, reassured But then the ground started to shake. The source of the tremor was only twenty feet from Kirkgordon. Turning his head he saw something wilder than anything he had seen before.

Farthington was no longer standing there. The figure in his place was at least a foot taller. Metamorphosis is something that people rarely imagine; they usually think only about the difference between what was and what is. Like the butterfly, we put the changes inside a cocoon, invisible to the normal world. There was no cocoon around what was happening here. First, the neck extended, clicking with each vertebrae extended in the spine. Swelling like a rapidly inflated balloon, the legs took on a proportion difficult to comprehend. Expanding and remoulding, the face's smooth human roundness was replaced with a sharpness of anger and hate. Despite hearing Austerley hit the ground in a faint, Kirkgordon couldn't take his eyes off an enormous sprouting tail which finally reached some ten feet. It was proportionate to the giant twenty-foot dragon that now graced the ground where Farthington had stood.

Time-lapsed nature films suddenly sprung into Kirkgordon's mind. This was particularly apt considering the way that two extra necks sprung out from the shoulders before a head manifested itself onto each of these writhing stems. All three heads now had an extended jaw, inside of which were forming sharpened teeth. Pointed ears emerged from the side of each head, and scales formed across the whole body of the beast. Yet Kirkgordon could still see, inset into the sockets of each visage, the eyes of Farthington. Kirkgordon's nerves were shot to pieces and he could feel his legs trembling. Deep in his core, the warrior spirit was yelling at him to stand and fight, but his mind was racing wildly.

The dragon that was Farthington now stood some twelve foot tall with heads that moved with abandon in front of and around each other. To see them was to see a melee of horror before your very eyes. Kirkgordon was transfixed with blackest wonder until a terrible cry broke the air.

"змей Горыныч, die!" yelled Calandra, throwing her jacket to the ground before her wings erupted from her back, spreading out to their full width of some ten feet. She took to the air in a charge at the dragon while spinning her staff with both hands until it began to glow white, forming a luminous circle. Kirkgordon stared at the impending collision and marvelled as the staff took one of the heads clean off at the neck. However, another head managed to grab Calandra's leg, whipping her upwards before letting her fly through the air behind the beast, crashing into a pile of broken-down vehicles. The beast turned towards her and its central head let off a blast of fire just to the left of Calandra, causing the truck's engine cowling to catch fire and burn with a dull orange. The dragon then walked towards its decapitated head, stooped down and let his wounded neck conjoin with its missing appendage. A swift and miraculous healing took place and by the time the neck had righted itself there was no wound to be seen. Turning again toward Calandra, the beast slowly moved in.

The terror inside Kirkgordon forced his brain into thought. He realized that the dragon believed Calandra had the manuscript. If not, surely she would have been fried by now. Calandra was lying groggy on the ground beside the burning truck. It was one of those moments when there is no sense, just a crazy plan and a wild hope. Blast it, here goes!

"Farthington!" Kirkgordon addressed the dragon. "You want the music sheet, I got it. If you want it, you'll need to rip this old pro apart to get it. And that ain't been done yet!" Except by those Nightgaunts, an inner voice murmured. It's never encouragement from the voices at these times, thought Kirkgordon. His address was having the desired effect; the great beast swung round to face him. The ground shook as the dragon rumbled forward and Kirkgordon prayed he had anticipated this right. He won't fry me. He knows I'll be looking for his heads to attack. So he'll use the other weapon. Come on big boy, Farthington keeps his weapons in the dark until he needs them. He's pure subterfuge. Come on.

The dragon was approximately ten feet from Kirkgordon when it suddenly stopped. Without any hesitation, it spun on its heels, whipping its huge tail around, the barbed end of which was sailing directly for Kirkgordon's head. Anticipation was everything and Kirkgordon was well ahead of this

Crescendo!

game. He ducked the flailing appendage and raced hard towards Calandra. She had landed on her back so the rolled-up manuscript tucked into the back of her trousers was not visible. On reaching Calandra, he slid into her and pushed her over onto her front before ripping the sheet music from her garments. He passed the manuscript from his right hand to his left as he quickly stood up again. The stomping footsteps of an irate dragon rang loud in his ears but he dared not stop to look. With his left hand he casually tossed the manuscript onto the burning hood of the truck where the dried parchment quickly started to blaze.

Gunshots are extreme to an eardrum but never had Kirkgordon heard such a sound as now emanated from the dragon. As he started to run he clasped his ears with his hands to protect them. Such a roar must have been heard from miles away. Kirkgordon was heading towards Austerley who was starting to stir, the roar bringing him back to consciousness. Behind Kirkgordon, the dragon's charge could be heard. As he was approaching Austerley, Kirkgordon heard the beast take in a large breath. Operating on pure instinct, his mind associated with this sound a plan of action and he grabbed a car door lying casually on the ground and skidded to a halt in front of Austerley. As he turned his head to face his foe the fiery blast was already on its way.

The ball of heat was nearly on him before he managed to place the car door in front of his unprotected body. It was only his shoes that caught fire but the searing heat came from all around. Austerley was more fortunate, as his distance behind the shield meant much of the blaze had dissipated by the time it reached him. Screaming at the pain, Kirkgordon managed to force his yell into a phrase. "Out! We need an out!"

Glancing over the top of his protective barrier, Kirkgordon saw the dragon advancing but he also saw Calandra on her knees drawing on the ground with the end of her staff. A hand grabbed his shoulder as an unsteady Austerley sought to seek shelter behind the hot and gently blazing car door. Fighting the pain in his feet, which were starting to blister, Kirkgordon desperately tried to form a plan to get back to Calandra. He hoped he knew what she was doing.

"Austerley, stay close and tight. Oh, and this is going to hurt!" The grip on his shoulder got stronger as Austerley took in the message. As the dragon formerly known as Farthington advanced, Kirkgordon, holding the car door in front of him, wheeled into his position. Suddenly he stopped.

"Churchy, keep moving! Bloody hell, keep moving! It'll fry us!" shouted Austerley.

"No, it won't," Kirkgordon stated calmly, "but it will whack us with that tail." It has to want the door off us, he thought. Please God, let me have this right! Within a blink of an eye, the tail came into Kirkgordon's upper right view and he braced himself for the collision. Austerley, however, was still drinking in Kirkgordon's last statement and promptly fainted at the thought of it. His body did not have time to hit the ground as he and his would-be protector were swept off their feet along with the car door, which was seeing more action now than it ever had in its vehicular life. The landing blow for Austerley would have been more substantial if not for his passive state, and he cushioned Kirkgordon's fall as well as that of the car door. Calandra's voice boomed and the end of her staff lit up. The markings she had drawn on the ground came alive with a shimmering white. She grabbed her friends by their necks, one with each hand, and hauled them inside the pattern she had drawn. Suddenly the ground swallowed them up. They were gone.

Chapter 11

Hangover Cures

Wednesday opening up was always a bit of a drag for Patrick Mahoney. This was due to the Tuesday night lock-in with the retired golfing community, which had become a permanent fixture during the last twelve months. Seamus Murphy was to blame. It was blasted Seamus who had cajoled him into shutting out the world until three a.m. that first time, thereby setting the standard for a normal early morning's entertainment. Unfortunately last night's had been a little more than normal.

Patrick grabbed a bottle of milk from the fridge and then poured himself a large glass, using the novelty rodent vessel his wife had brought him back from the family's trip to that damnable theme park.

Meandering to the door, checking on the ashes from the previous night's fire, he opened it with a tepid push and forced his way out into the blinding sunlight. Being late December, there was a heavy chill in the air, although the nearby coast did help hold it just above freezing. There were two locals waiting by the door. These brothers, well known in this tiny village, miles from anywhere, were regular early morning fixtures, tied by invisible bonds to the liquor.

"Morning lads," said Patrick, to little response. Although his eyes were squinting, Patrick swore he could see other figures just down the road. One, two, oh and a third. And the third was a woman; things were looking up!

"Hello there!" shouted Patrick to the oncoming group. "Lovely morning for a stroll." As the group started to come into focus, he was able to see that they had had a rough night too. The woman was hobbling and the men looked like they had taken a severe beating. Indeed, there was even a whiff of something in the air. Like charcoal, a burnt burger smell. Hadn't Murphy said old Fitzgerald was entertaining some foreigners up at the estate last night? Strange crowd for him though. "Was it rough at Fitzgerald's last night?" he asked.

"Fitzgerald's? What the hell are you on about?" The rebuttal came from the man in the centre of the group, who was obviously bruised about his face, with cuts plastering his forehead and cheeks. "Churchy, where are we?"

"Alive somewhere, that's where! And if you ever

run off ahead again I'll break your legs and wheel you about in future." The other gentleman, whose eyes, Patrick noticed, were constantly scanning all around, extended a hand towards the pub owner. "Bout ye! Where are we in Ireland?"

"That must have been some night, my friend. Thirtyacres. Near Galway. The village is basically the pub. Me name's Patrick. Patrick Mahoney."

"Kirkgordon, Patrick. Nice to meet you. These are my friends, Austerley and Cally. And yes, it was a bit of a night."

"Good to meet you, Kirk. Anything I can get for you?"

"Sure. Paracetamol, full packet if possible. And a coffee, a Guinness and a jug of water."

"The Guinness for you?"

"They're all for me. You guys want something?"

Patrick listened to the orders: egg roll, vodka and orange juice for the lady, a large tumbler of rum, neat, for the other man and anything fried that could fill a plate. Oh well, it was business.

Returning some fifteen minutes later with a large tray, Patrick found his customers sitting on the wooden benches outside the pub in a state of undress. The woman was sat down minus her trousers with Kirk exercising her left leg, her face in a grimace. Patrick was careful not to be too overt in his appreciation of her looks as she appeared to be a woman who could handle herself. Kirk had his top off and it looked like he had washed in the nearby trough. Austerley was standing in just his underpants, inspecting the bottom of his backside, which had a deep cut. The rest of his body was heavily bruised and scarred and he had obviously partaken of the water in the trough too.

"There you go. We do have rooms with showers. You should've said." Smiling broadly, Patrick left the tray on one of the wooden tables beside the benches. Oh well, it takes all sorts. "I'll be inside if you need anything else."

"Okay, cheers," Kirkgordon replied, without looking up from Calandra's leg. "There's nothing broke, Cally. Might take a while to get that bruising down though."

Calandra nodded and reached for her trousers. Jumping up onto her good leg, she pulled them over the other leg before sitting down again to place the good leg inside. Damn, she's light on her feet, thought Kirkgordon. Looking across to Austerley, he was relieved to see that a relatively normal state of dress had been resumed. Kirkgordon pulled on his top and sat down to neck his Guinness before dropping some paracetamol with his coffee. He felt rough; but inside, he was relieved just to be alive. His brain, processing the image of a man turning into a dragon, attacked him with images of fire and great swishing tails.

"You know, burning it was pretty pointless. It's just going to reappear, and in a fashion that's a whole lot easier to find. There's no way we can find it first!" grumbled Austerley.

"Well, I would have asked, if somebody hadn't dropped to the ground like a sack of potatoes!" snapped Kirkgordon in return. "I would have thought you'd have got used to stuff like this by now, after all, it's what you keep seeking."

"I was just a smidgeon woozy after the beating I took from Farthington."

"Yeah, but all he did was turn into a dragon. Throwing fire around. I mean, it's your sort of party!"

"No," interrupted Calandra, "he didn't turn into a dragon. He turned back from being a man."

"What the hell are you on about?" asked Kirkgordon, his eyes widening in growing horror.

"She's right," confirmed Austerley. "Heck of a disguise though. That was Zmey Gorynych. Never thought I would meet him."

"Grand! Now you can tick that one off in your big-scary-monsters-of-doom scrap book. You're actually proud of it. Un-flipping-real!"

"Churchy, that was a good call," Calandra interrupted, trying to calm the situation down. "Zmey is a mercenary. He wouldn't want the manuscript for himself, but he has ways of obtaining things that are out of earthly reach. Now it's no longer out of reach, so I doubt we will see him again."

"A mercenary? How?" asked Kirkgordon in disbelief.

"What do dragons like? Gold, treasure. So, he's a clever one with a talent for changing shape. Yes, he's a mercenary. But he's not our problem any more."

"No, he's not," Austerley took up, "but the manuscript's whereabouts is. They asked me about certain rituals. Well, actually, they used drugs and other devices to elicit certain facts and practices. They needed things from my head but I can't remember the conversations. Just some of the pain. There is a sense of foreboding though."

"A what? A sense of foreboding? Awesome, Indy! Top spy you are! Bond would be..."

"Shut up!" Calandra jumped in. "For what? My darling, for what?" she said, suddenly breaking into the Russian voice that Austerley loved. They stood looking at Austerley, who was motionless, but obviously searching deep into the recesses of his mind. Eventually he spoke, but his voice was quiet and trembling.

"A summoning. Something horrible. Destruction and death. Something not from here. Something... something... something... black!"

Kirkgordon looked at Calandra, shaking his head gently.

"Take a few of these, Indy," he said, handing over the paracetamol.

"No! He needs a computer. Internet, now," insisted Calandra, "while he has the sense. Let him find it!"

Chapter 12

Internet Connections

It had taken negotiation and some upfront cash to persuade Patrick Mahoney to forgo his bedroom, kicking his wife out in the process. Actually, it was a credit card, for which Mr Mahoney had a reader. Kirkgordon was not too happy about this, fearing that their current whereabouts would be compromised, but Calandra was insistent. They had been ushered past the quite put-out wife and had heard the snide and snappy exchanges that had commenced once the bedroom door was shut. Having led Austerley, who was still in a state of trance, into the room, Calandra now sat him on the plain wooden chair in front of the outdated computer. A pair of knickers obscuring the screen were quickly cast aside, then all eyes turned to Austerley, who just sat there.

"So what's he meant to do? Can you find his on switch?" urged Kirkgordon, mindful of the cost of this connection.

"Shush!" rebuked Calandra, before gently pushing Kirkgordon away until they had reached the back wall. "He needs to focus and he doesn't need a smarmy idiot getting in the way," she whispered.

Kirkgordon was taken aback by the force of her dismissal.

Calandra saw the hurt in Kirkgordon's eyes. "Dammit, Churchy! It's not about that. He just needs some space. He's linked, you see. They put him under and connected him with the manuscript. He was tied into it, became part of its future. And now he's retained some of that. It's not unusual. At least, it wasn't the last time I saw this. Four hundred years ago, give or take a decade. Just stay here and watch. Don't be upset. There's no one to save here. No big rescue, no one to protect. This is his world, let him walk in it. And he needs my help."

Again she saw Kirkgordon's eyes drop. Part of Calandra raged. She had offered herself and he had refused, no, not refused, merely done the right thing, held out hope for his lost love and protected her from her own insecurity. She felt the burning passion too, but he had no right to be like this. Still, she knew she would have been hurting the same. So she gently kissed him on the lips. He lifted his eyes to her and she swore she saw the hint of a tear before he waved her back to Austerley.

Meanwhile, Austerley was typing. This was not unusual, except that his eyes were closed and his head was turned almost one hundred and eighty degrees from the screen. His body was agitated. Constant involuntary reactions peppered his frame and he gave out a low drone as he typed. Kirkgordon raised his eyes as he watched Calandra stand behind Austerley and gently stroke the back of his neck. She whispered into his ear as dozens of different websites appeared on the screen. Then, suddenly, Austerley keeled over, fell off the chair and would have hit the floor if not for Calandra's quick reactions.

"Is he all right?" asked Kirkgordon.

"Relatively... yes, relatively," came Calandra's cryptic response. Austerley was quickly awake, possibly from the jolt of Calandra's catch, and he sat back up and stared at the screen.

"Sorry. Sorry... they blocked me. Someone blocked me." Austerley's head hung low.

"It's okay, you did good. Didn't he?" Calandra prompted Kirkgordon.

He knew what the answer should be, knew he needed to encourage Austerley, but his frustration and anger at the situation he had found himself in got the better of him.

"Is that it?" he said, looking at the screen. "Some bloody auction site? Guess you were on AM not FM, certainly not digital!"

"Nice! Cheers for that," hissed Calandra. Men, she thought, always the same. Jealous when no reason exists. I'm not the one with a spouse!

"Sorry," whimpered Austerley, "it's where I got to."

Kirkgordon stared at the screen. Sommerline Auction Houses. It was a page outlining an auction to be held in two days' time near the village of Great Malvern in England, close to the Welsh border. It seemed quite small-scale, operating from a converted old chapel with only about a hundred items for sale. Marvellous, thought Kirkgordon. All his life, Indy's been touched, and now that we need it, he's lost the connection.

Part of him was relieved. This whole escapade was getting out of hand, certainly out of his depth. He had seen things recently that were not good for a man's constitution or mental stability. There was a growing attraction to Calandra, built on their interdependence in this fiasco, and he knew he was enjoying it. He needed to get away, get clear, visit the kids and see Alana again. They say the ripples of life can move people apart. What about tsunamis?

"There!" Austerley was pointing directly at the screen at a most grotesque painting. The graphic was small but was obviously of a creature in the throes of consuming something else.

"Austerley, that's disgusting. Get your sick mind off it and see if you can tune in to the vibe." Kirkgordon was on the edge of tipping and didn't need Austerley indulging himself in grotesque fantasy.

"I used to own that. It's a classic!"

"What do you mean? And, anyway, do I care? Get back on the program and find that manuscript!" thundered Kirkgordon.

"But it's a Pickman! Stunning, just stunning. You can't beat live models."

"I don't care if it's a damn Picasso! It's not what we are looking for, so get on with the search before they track us through the credit card." Kirkgordon shook his head furiously and walked to the back of the room to avoid lamping Austerley round the ears. It's always a game to him, isn't it? Oh, look at this monster, look at that spawn of evil, can I get a word with that undead thing? A whole big game to him. Then the horror of Austerley's response hit him.

"Live? What do you mean, live?" Kirkgordon planted his face right in front of Austerley's. "How do you do a live version of that? Invite them round for coffee and biscuits and casually ask them to stand over there a moment? Oh, by the way, there's a little snack on the floor. Feel free to munch away while I paint this."

"But it's Pickman!" announced an exasperated Austerley. "You met him, in the alley in Moscow."

"Sorry, what are you on about?"

"In the alley. Okay, so he's not the handsome man he used to be, but it was Pickman. He gave us the time of the street's arrival."

"Handsome? He wasn't even a man!"

"Well, no, he's technically a ghoul of some sort, I guess."

"Technically?"

"Pickman? *The* Pickman?" Calandra chirped in.

"Oh, I see, he's one of the family. Not an Adams, is he?" fumed Kirkgordon.

"Don't be a prick! This is important," Calandra spat back. Then she took a hand to the back of Kirkgordon's neck, rubbing it soothingly. "This could be it, Churchy. Pickman is a high interest person... sorry, thing... in the darker places. You don't see this type of painting in an open auction." The neck rub felt good despite the icy touch. Kirkgordon was disappointed at how easily she redirected him, but he loved the caress.

"Okay, okay. So what does this mean?" Her hand was still on his neck.

"I don't know," came the slow, ponderous answer from Austerley.

"No connection at all. Any hints?"

"Sorry Churchy, no. I got the information about the street from Pickman and now I am drawn to one of his paintings. That's it. Pickman's not a player. He didn't even want to know about the manuscript. In life, he was an artist who was able to befriend the... creatures of the night, shall we say, and paint them. His work was shockingly real but no one back then realized they were real life portraits. And now he's a ghoul, all this stuff means so little to him. Sad, really."

"Not the word I would have chosen. I mean, that thing is eating something else in the picture. Sounds evil to me. Trust you to have held a picture of his." Kirkgordon wondered what to do. All links except this one are gone, he thought. There's an evil rising of some sort but who knows what? And she's still rubbing my neck.

"Guess it's time to see his work close up. Get the address and let's go, we're going to have to push it to make it in time." Kirkgordon saw a smile on Austerley's face and heard him say under his breath "a real Pickman again".

He's too close to it all, Kirkgordon thought. Indy is too steeped in it to see the evil, the wrongness. He stared intently as Austerley exited the room.

"Thank you," said Calandra.

"For what?"

"For keeping going. You could have just walked," she whispered. She tilted her head and kissed him gently on the lips. That bitter chill stung again but this time it ran down his tongue too. And now she pushed hard up against him before forcing his mouth open with her tongue. He tasted her crisp tongue before quickly drawing back.

"And they say *I'm* frosty!" she said.

"Was that for me, or for the... mission-thing we are on?" They were inches from each other. Kirkgordon fought every impulse coursing through him to take her in his arms right then. The thrill of the moment and the excitement of such a wondrous, albeit strange, woman overwhelmed his senses.

"I don't prostitute myself for causes." It was said firmly but deliberately, confirming Kirkgordon's fears.

"Then please stop, Calandra. I'm not that strong." Gently he broke away, seeing her pain as he headed for the door.

Chapter 13

Girl Talk

"Isn't she fantastic?"

Kirkgordon nodded gently without glancing at "her". Austerley nudged him and pointed abruptly with his eyes. Flicking his head sharply in Calandra's direction, Kirkgordon grunted, before restoring his attention to the in-flight magazine. It had been a rush to get to Dublin for the flight to Cardiff and Kirkgordon was trying to focus his mind on what was ahead by immersing himself in the minutiae of the free copy in his lap. Fortunately, there were no adjacent seats in which they could all sit and so Calandra was four rows forward, the emergency exit seat allowing her to stretch out her leg. Austerley was clear of his trance state and seemed keen to tell in much deeper detail his previous encounters with Calandra.

"That was something else in the restaurant, though. That voice of hers... oh, it drives me wild, that does. She was always so dark, mysterious and sensual. And the kinkiness of that touch. I tell you, when she's flesh on flesh..."

"Indy, shut it. Please. Whatever sordid little games or deviant practices you got up to, I don't want to know. She's a fellow, eh... warrior, or squad member, team player... ah... yeah, whatever, so I don't need to think of her like that. Keep the sordid details to yourself."

"All right, no need to be so abrupt. Probably surprised you that she went for someone like me, though. She can see through people, you see, bit of an inner judge. Knows a good egg."

"Yes, you're lovely, okay! Focus on what's ahead."

"Are you looking forward to it?"

Kirkgordon turned his head with a start. His quizzical look failed to stop Austerley from launching into a speech like an acolyte talking of his master.

"Think of it, Churchy. One of the big ones turning up. One of the Elder beings. Dreadfully impressive, something no one, or at least very few, have ever seen before. One of the earliest visitors to our planet coming back. Think of the power in those hands, the unrequited purpose of a thousand years, the..."

"You sound like an American voice-over artist.

Get a grip. If things are as bad as that book says... well, this might be it!'" Help me God if it is, thought Kirkgordon. And this idiot beside me wants to charge right in and take a look. Probably bring his camera. And his spotter's guide. Oh, look, it's a Pickman! Maybe he'll...

Kirkgordon watched Austerley get up and force his way past him through the incredibly narrow gap so often described as leg room. Fortunately, the image of Austerley's backside dissipated quickly, especially when replaced by the sight of Calandra walking towards him from her seat.

"Hey. You okay?" she whispered gently. Kirkgordon nodded. "I'm sorry," she said.

"Don't be. If I wasn't a mentally unstable father of two with a wife, albeit an estranged one, your advances would have worked. But I can't handle this now. Especially with Austerley wanting to brag about your past activities. We need to lay it to one side. Sorry."

"Okay," came the whispered response and she kissed him gently on the forehead, allowing him a glance at her torso. Dammit, thought Kirkgordon, she can't be in such close proximity.

"Where the hell is this all leading, Cally? The Elder thing, I mean. Where will it take us?"

"It's very deep stuff. Things don't leave that sort of resonance normally, even in someone as open to it as Austerley. I'm scared, Churchy. The last time I saw something like this, a whole town was obliterated by a single presence. Only a wise holy man could stop it. And this reaction of Austerley's is far greater than what happened back then. I'm scared." Calandra bowed her head in front of Kirkgordon and he could see the faintest tremble of her shoulders.

"How much can Austerley help? He's like a child in a sweet shop. He's actually keen on meeting this whatever."

"You need to watch him, for he is a child. He craves the mystery, the power, the drama of it all. Remember none of what you see will be good. It is pure evil. It tempts and then destructs. Watch him closely. He is our expert, but he's also theirs!"

"Go sit down, Cally. We all need a little rest, while it's not raining." She looked at him, wondering at the expression. "Sorry. The flood doesn't grow when the rain's stopped," Kirkgordon clarified.

"You expect a flood?"

Kirkgordon laughed. "Not of the water variety. But yes, there's a dam about to break."

Chapter 14

Bidding Frenzy

Four countries in a day, thought Kirkgordon. Russia, Ireland, plane to Wales and now over the border to England. Stepping out of the taxi, Kirkgordon surveyed the greyish building in front of him. It was once a small English church but now housed auctions and other small functions. The arched windows, the grey slate, the sloping roof, all combined with the cross-shaped design that was typical of many churches Kirkgordon had stood in on this island. There was a distinct classical beauty to the parish church but he feared for the sanctity of the interior. While he was gazing at this former bastion of village life, Austerley roughly brushed past him, eager to see the articles available for sale.

Or, rather, one particular article. Kirkgordon felt a touch of anger at Indy's lack of respect for this sacred ground, but a gentle touch on his arm brought him to his senses. A smiling Calandra took his hand and led him from the fading winter's afternoon into the glare of artificial light.

An aged, white-haired, short but stout woman handed Kirkgordon a brochure at the door. He ignored it, preferring to scan the small crowd of people inside. Wielding a small gavel in his left hand was a small but efficient man with glasses, sporting a bright bow tie which sat at the jauntiest of angles. A drab audience failed to rise to the impassioned callings of the man, who was telling the history of a morose-looking statue of a duck. Kirkgordon watched Austerley flick rapidly through the brochure, eventually finding his prize.

"Number one-four-five. Just made it, Churchy. That's one-four-three being bid on at the moment."

"No phone bidders, anyway. That's good," said Calandra. Kirkgordon noted her arm in his and indicated his surprise with his eyes. "It's for the look of the thing. Cheer up!" She pecked him on the cheek. Austerley's glower was unnoticed by Calandra but not Kirkgordon. Bugger, he thought.

The purchasing crowd was nondescript, with most people dressed casually. Warm winter coats and scarves lay across the seats of the half-empty room which was lit by an overcompensation of LED lights powered by a droning generator outside. So many of these old churches were without heating or electricity and the damp on the walls told a sorry tale. Kirkgordon thought of Jesus standing amongst the merchants in the temple courts, and he longed to turn over the tables. Somewhere deep inside, his almost-expired faith was rekindling, not least in reaction to his present troubles. He felt he needed someone "big" on his side. And almost immediately he apologized to the "big" one for such a flippant description of Him.

"Look! Over there!" said Austerely.

"Are you serious, Indy? It's not exactly a wall-filler, is it?" remarked Kirkgordon.

"Well no, Mr Picasso, it's not. But it's the genuine thing. One hundred percent Pickman. Perfect in every detail. Used to look divine over my mantelpiece. Had a set of lamps to make sure you got the full effect from it."

"Full effect? Bloody hell, Austerley. And divine? It's gross, disgusting... repugnant... and evil."

"Little bit quick on the judgement, Churchy. Just because something's not to your taste doesn't make it evil!"

"I'm calling it evil because that creature appears to be having a taste of something else. Pickman's unreal! How is he so blind? Look at it. I mean look at it! It's just damn disgusting and sick! Who would want to capture a creature like that, never mind paint it?" asked Kirkgordon.

"Okay, if I can just get a word in past Picasso and Da Vinci for a moment, I guess you're both right. It's certainly perfect in every detail," said Calandra.

"There! See, Churchy, it's a masterpiece."

"Cally? What do you mean, in every detail?" She didn't flinch but Kirkgordon could see that her memories were reaching out from deep recesses.

"Every detail. Every single scale and point on its flesh. The sinewy but lethally explosive legs with those sharp hooks at the end. The hands, deepest green. Oh, and they hit like a sledgehammer. That throat, seemingly weak but so very hard to strangle. And those eyes. Evil, like you said. The eyes, those windows to the soul. That's Christian, ain't it, Churchy? If I hadn't got to the eyes... it would have had me! So yeah, trust me. He might have been a mad bastard, but Pickman could paint."

Austerley reached out a hand to her shoulder but Calandra brushed it aside. Both men watched her back disappear towards the ladies' restroom.

"Bit touchy!"

"Dammit, Austerley! Not everyone enjoys the circus of freaks."

"Freaks, is it? Mental cases, nut jobs, cranky arses like myself?"

"She's been thrown into it. Don't judge her to be one of them by her looks."

"The expert on female freaks now, are you? Gonna redeem her, save her from my kind? I think you're getting a taste for the freakish flesh, I think you... argh!" Suddenly, Austerley crumpled to the floor, clutching his knee. Despite the pain, he whipped his head round to glare at Kirkgordon with obvious anger. A few of the gathered bidders offered Austerley a helping hand but he waved them away, rising in a semi-manly fashion before turning and limping away.

Oh hell, Kirkgordon thought. Circus of freaks. Bollocks!

Suddenly the numbers one, four and five drew his attention. The auctioneer, with professional glee, was calling out the next exhibit. Bet he doesn't describe it as perfect! Eyes and ears, Kirkgordon reminded himself. Scan. Scan hard. When the picture was shown to the audience there was an audible intake of breath and the occasional "disgusting" and "what's that shite?" Undaunted, the auctioneer announced his intention to seek an opening bid of at least two hundred pounds.

"He'll be lucky." The quiet female voice came from over Kirkgordon's shoulder and was followed by arms encircling his waist. His body eased into the wrap with the greatest delight while his brain screamed at him to run for cover. Pulled back by years of routine, he continued his scan and spotted Austerley staring his way, incensed, his features forming a bullish rebuke. His friend spun round and instantly threw an arm into the air.

"What's he doing? Churchy, what's he at?" Calandra asked.

"Hell have no fury like a lunatic scorned. Bollocks!" replied Kirkgordon.

I can't tell her about the little tête-à-tête, he thought. She's looking for comfort after the shock of that picture. But I can't, dammit, she'll take it as a come-on. She'll think I'm okay with it. This sort of crap is why I used to work alone. It was easier to detach when they paid you the money.

"Two hundred, on my right," said the auctioneer.

"What? Hey, what's the big deal? Thought you would like a cuddle?" Calandra said.

"Not now! We're working. See if there's a rival bidder."

"Two hundred and fifty."

"Where's that, Cally?"

"Two seventy-five."

"Tell Austerley to keep his flamin' hand down for two seconds 'til I see where he's pointing!"

"Was only a cuddle?"

"Three hundred!"

"Not now! Black hat, is that him?"

"Three twenty-five, sir?"

"Okay, let's see if we can't get round him."

"Three twenty-five it is..."

"Cane, black suit, short cropped hair. Got him!"

"Against you, sir?"

"Shadow him, but close."

"No bid, sir? It's against you, three twenty-five."

"Why's he not bidding, Churchy? Austerley's going to win this!"

"Arse!"

"Four hundred pounds! New bidder! Four hundred pounds, thank you, sir."

"Where Cally, where?"

"Five hundred!" The buzz amongst the audience was growing as the expected price range of one to three hundred pounds was being smashed to smithereens. Sweat was pouring down the face of the auctioneer now; he was elated, and he was driving every ounce of feeling into every call.

"Six hundred! Ladies and gentlemen, six hundred pounds to the rugged warrior on my right. Very brave sir, very brave."

"He's gonna be pleased with that description."

"Cally, friggin' find the guy. Stop gawking and get working!"

"Seven hundred! The lady with the rather fine large bangle earrings. Seven hundred."

"Got her! Have you got her? Beside the man in the blue jacket! Yes, him."

"One thousand! For Mr Pickman's finest."

"Bloody hell, love, the guy's insane. A grand for that abomination. It's like a dog ripping a fox!" shouted an onlooker.

"Cally, stay with her. I need to shut Indy up!"

"Two thousand! To our bangled lady towards the back. Back on you sir! At two thousand pounds."

"Indy, bloody stop it, now. I don't want to make a scene. We have her. Drop out! Let's pick her up outside."

"Piss off! I'm a freak, you ain't gonna stop me!"

"Anything further, sir? At you at two thous... Three thousand pounds!"

"Dammit, Austerley, I didn't want to do this."

"Four thousand! Thank you, dear lady, four thousand pounds."

"Do whatever you..."

"At you sir? My goodness, he's dropped like a sack of potatoes. Are you okay, sir? He's fine, you say. It's all right everyone, our friend's just got a little too excited. His friend says he's okay. Wow! Four thousand pounds, I'm a little excited myself.

Anyone else? At four thousand pounds... once... twice... and for the last time at four thousand pounds... sold!"

Kirkgordon breathed a sigh of relief and crouched down on one knee, cradling Austerley. There were legs and well-wishing faces all around, so he was just going to have to go on trust that Calandra would tail the item winner. Damn Austerley, every time!

Nerve pinching was something Kirkgordon had learned in his previous employment. It had come in handy on occasion, more often on a client who protested his chosen course of action than on an enemy. He wondered how Austerley would react on waking up, something he hoped would happen soon, as Indy was a heavy man. He rolled Indy's arm around his own neck and, with significant effort, carried him from the room, feet dragging along the floor. Outside, he plonked him on a wooden bench and carefully held his neck until he had settled into an upright sleeping position.

"Good afternoon, sir. Kindly refrain from moving, I'd hate to shoot you."

It was Farthington's voice. What the hell did he want now? Damn, thought Kirkgordon, I hope he doesn't need something from Austerley's head. Calandra's not even here to run cover.

"That's good. Very good of you to see sense. Really no need for any excitement here. I'm just here to talk. Just a few questions."

Kirkgordon slowly turned his head to try to look at Farthington and was surprised no one checked this tactic. And there he was, Farthington. No. Hang on. It was the man who had put in the initial bid on the painting. That hat. He does look somewhat like Farthington. Less stocky. But the same voice. Or at least, so very close.

"Farthington? Is that you, Zmey Gorynych?"

"Farthington is a name one is unacquainted with. But Zmey Gorynych? How do you know him? Paying over the odds for a Pickman and now keeping company with dragons? You would appear rather unconventional for the company you keep. Kindly turn and face me. That's better. Just a quick picture for the boys back home. No smile, but it will do."

The gentleman holding Kirkgordon in check was pointing a gun, held in his left hand, at Kirkgordon's forehead. The other hand was busy texting, or something similar, with the phone that had taken the picture. He's too far back, Kirkgordon thought. I'll never reach him before he plants a bullet in my skull. I'm not sure he would hesitate, either.

"Ah! The boys back home are somewhat good at this kind of thing. Some days you do get delays but not today, Mr Kirkgordon. I assume that is Mr Austerley sat asleep beside you. Or is he slightly incapacitated? Trouble with the troops, eh? Is the lady with you?"

Kirkgordon didn't flinch at any of this information. Instead he chose to remain quiet, awaiting his enemy's next move.

"Oh, sorry! Forgive me," said the man, dropping

his gun in the process. "Major Arthur Lewis Siddlington-Havers, at your service. But you can call me Havers. From Her Majesty's finest, if least known, department."

"Havers, you may well be telling the truth but someone conned me before so can I see some sort of ID?"

"Well of course, sir, but exactly what type of ID would suit yourself? Paper, hologram, blood? Let's see if we can find something." He started tapping on his phone again.

"My deepest pardons but I have need of you," he spoke into the phone. "Just a word please, he'll have work to do. Thank you, Mrs Kirkgordon." Havers held the phone out for Kirkgordon who stared at it like it was the finest of whiskies. He knew this was going to be good but what the consequences would be, who knew?

"Als? That really you?"

"Yes Mr C, it is. He found you, thank God."

"What's up? Are you okay? The kids?"

"We're fine! Totally fine! In hiding, but fine."

"Hiding? Why? Who? Damn! What the hell's happening?"

"I don't know exactly, C, but they got us out. Police at first, then these people. SETA."

"SETA? What the blazes is that?"

"Let him tell you. Shit, I'm trembling, C. He got you, that's all that counts."

"As long as you're okay, Als! Stay safe!"

"I'm sorry, Mr Kirkgordon, but I can't risk that location being traced."

"Gotta go, Als. Dammit, I miss you. I will get better for you."

"I know, C. I know. Don't get killed."

"No. No, I won't." And he hung up.

Kirkgordon held onto the phone for a moment, staring at it, before looking up at a small party arriving. Several men in suits were flanking Calandra, who looked relieved to see him.

"Hey, the cavalry's turned up then. Havers, long time. Churchy, are you okay?" she asked.

"Yes... yes, fine," Kirkgordon replied. Alana had sounded concerned. She wanted him, clearly, hopefully, maybe. Please God, all I needed was five minutes on the phone. Explain this one to me. Just typical. I can't get to be with Alana, yet I can't get away from the siren... no, that's unfair... the woman who is turning all my sense dials to the max. It's just crap! And Austerley's going to be pissed at me when he wakes. Never mind the end of the world, I'm a social pariah on heat!

"Are you okay, Mr Kirkgordon?" Havers ventured, watching him from a sombre, contemplative pose.

"Yeah, fine! Who the hell's SETA?"

"Smith, get the limo round. We can talk on the way, Mr Kirkgordon. I take it Mr Austerley will not need assistance in waking up? Good. I can bring you up to speed on the way to the pub. We have important notes to compare and not that long to do it. I fear a cataclysmic event may be in the offing."

"So I keep hearing."

Chapter 15

The Government Agent

Austerley was awake enough to accept a large brandy in the back of the limo. Sitting opposite Kirkgordon, his mood never lightened and he emitted dark looks from under furrowed eyebrows. Calandra was actually in buoyant mood, having succeeded in her part of the mission. Havers' arrival was a turn-up for the books and a bit of luxury travel was suiting her still-aching leg. The debate began between the four would-be saviours of the planet.

"Mr Kirkgordon, you came up on the radar in Russia but the FSB were struggling to track you. They did find you once but apparently this dear lady was too much of a match for them. More brandy,

Mr Austerley?" Havers was chuffed to bits too, just in a more eloquent way.

"Yes! Hell, yes! What did you do to me?" said Austerley, glaring intensely at Kirkgordon.

"Nerve pinch. Stops a lot of deadly foes. And the odd arsehole."

"Now then, gentlemen," intervened Havers, "there are more pressing things at hand, I fear. As I was saying, we heard about your exploits in Russia and then the countryside altercation. Then total silence. The FSB, and I have to admit ourselves also, believed that something had got to you out in the sticks. But I understand now that Calandra was showing her worth. Always a good stick, Calandra. Top notch on a tricky wicket."

"Churchy seems to think so, anyway." Having delivered the low blow, Austerley turned his face to the window. Havers ignored this and continued.

"We picked up on certain occurrences too. Lots of activity around selected items. And what with Mr Austerley possibly being with a hostile force, we thought best to protect certain individuals, and hence we took measures to have your family secured, Mr Kirkgordon." Calandra's face dropped. She hadn't been expecting the competition to still be around.

"That's why you were there today?" Kirkgordon queried.

"Is this for the slow kids not keeping up? Dammit, Churchy, you didn't get the brains, did you?"

Crescendo!

"Enough, Austerley! Grow up. Just cos she hasn't got the hots for you any more, don't bring it into everything." Damn, thought Kirkgordon, that wasn't the moment. Deserved, but not the moment. Cally's not going to enjoy that.

"Boys! In case you're wondering, this old girl's had about enough of the pair of you. Maybe you could behave a bit more like Major Havers. Do continue, Arthur. Let's get onto the important matters."

"Gladly, dear lady, gladly. When we saw all this activity occurring we decided to try and get in, in front of the targets. It has taken some time and a bit of luck but we managed it today. Previously, we missed a copy of Zahn's manuscript being sold in Zurich and a small Elder conducting baton changing hands in Boston. We think it may be the same buyer, but they are doing it through various different hands. Fortunately, we captured a source today and with a little persuasion we have obtained an address. Ah, here we are! The base. One of Her Majesty's Air Force bases. I promised a pub but the officer's mess will have to do. Draught on tap I believe. Even got the local brew. Damn fine dark. Mild, too, if you would prefer. One always has a dark."

The limo doors were opened and Havers led his motley gathering inside the green, dashed mess building. The room was empty except for a single barman dressed in his finest white and black bow tie. Pictures of regiments and aircraft lined the walls and a number of solid but rather bland oak-coloured tables occupied the floor. Four chairs sat around each table and Havers pulled one out for Calandra.

"G&T, dear lady?"

"Perfect, Major."

"Gentlemen?"

"Dark for me. Austerley's is a mild with a chaser. Malt mind, no crap."

"I can speak for myself, if you can keep that too-well-thought-of mouth under wraps. Major Havers, a pint of the finest mild and a dram of the single malt closest to the barman."

"Very good, gentlemen."

"And Havers?"

"Yes, Mr Kirkgordon?"

"I'll repeat my earlier question. Who is SETA?"

"SETAA, sir, S-E-T-A-A, is one of Her Majesty's lesser known but highly dedicated departments. And ever since you followed Mr Austerley down that grave near the Gainsville Pike we have been keeping a damn good eye on you both. Supernatural and Elder Threat Assessment Agency. We are not large in number and, indeed, most of our employees are, so to speak, freelance, but we have the ear of the top brass."

"The Joint Military Command?" ventured Austerley.

"A good deal higher than that!"

"Number ten?" said Kirkgordon, duelling to be one up.

"Prime ministers come and prime ministers go. Her Majesty is our head."

"So are you, like, MI5 then?"

"Mr Austerley, sometimes it would be prudent to take one at his word. Now, enough about where I come from and who I work for. The more pertinent question... there you go my dear... is exactly where you two stand. The dear lady I have had dealings with before and I know where her loyalty lies; despite hailing from outside these shores, she does stand for the good of mankind. As for yourselves, gentlemen, your track record is somewhat tainted. Let's take that graveyard for a start."

"That was his fault! All his bloody fault!" Kirkgordon protested. "I was running standard protection duty and this arse takes me down the hole of hell, just to get a glance at something of Carter's. Bloody nightmares, a back that's scored like a pork belly on Sunday and a rift between me and the missus that three months of therapy didn't even begin to touch. That was his baby. He dragged me in, and if it wasn't for me, we would have been dragged under!"

"There was a good chance to find items that would have led to Carter. It was over a hundred years, how was I to know they would still be there? And then you had to start shooting your pistols. Now you just shoot your mouth off," Austerley responded.

"Hold it there you... oh, thank you Havers. It was all you, Indy! You know it. We know it. There's only one thing that drives you. You're just like Carter!"

"A fact I am all too aware of, Mr Kirkgordon," interrupted Havers. "Now, just so we understand each other and understand how this relationship will work..."

"Relationship?"

"Yes, Mr Austerley, relationship. The relationship between yourselves and oneself. Now, we are all aware of your evasion of the FSB in Russia and a reliable source tells me that they are interested in whoever incapacitated one of their men in a metal container." Austerley chuckled, as Havers continued. "Their interest seems even deeper in a certain gentleman who was seen evading them from a restaurant and who is believed to have helped in securing a potentially dangerous document for an unknown power and unwisely passing on secrets about said document. Also, our American friends are looking for a certain inmate from a very select asylum taken by a charlatan for an unknown purpose. This particular character is of interest now to Her Majesty's Government as he was recently seen trying to purchase material believed to be required by a covert organization for a possible world-ending event. So yes, Mr Austerley, our relationship, in which I will direct and you will follow said directions, are we clear?"

"Nailed to your cross then," said Kirkgordon. "I hope you believe in redemption and forgiveness too, Havers?"

"I believe in protecting this land of mine and we will be working together to secure that purpose. Now, all primed? Then cheers!"

Havers took a measured draught of his dark and looked intently at his new compatriots. Turning to the bar, he quietly asked the barman to leave, watching him exit before turning back to the assembly. His driver, Smith, who stood guarding the entrance, was the only other person in the room.

"So, now I need everything you know about what is to come. Why Zahn's music? Why a conductor's baton? Why Pickman paintings? Nightgaunts in Russia? And plenty of other darker beings protecting other artefacts. All being gathered together by whom? And why a cryptic message from the lips of the man who seized the baton for me? Have cheer, it will topple. What is happening, friends?"

"Austerley had the sense for a while, Havers. That's how we tracked down the painting. The music was being sourced and found. As to what is going on, we haven't any specifics, we are just following a smell in the wind." Calandra swung her hair round clear of her face. "But it reeks of something Elder. A disturbance, judging how Austerley reacted. A rising of some sort. Remember the last time a statuette was found."

"What happened?" Suddenly Kirkgordon felt like he was the only one who had missed class. Havers and Austerley looked aside, embarrassed, while Calandra enlightened him.

"Basically, certain individuals decided that bringing back one of these Elder gods would be a good idea. Or rather, allowing him to rise. They believe that these creatures exist in the deep waiting to be set free. The last time one rose, the world got lucky. The person that witnessed it believed they collapsed it by ramming it with a boat, but the word today is that other factors may have been in play."

"They came from outer space, have been here from ancient times and first formed us," added Austerley.

"Wait right there. Formed us? Only one person formed us and he's the one thing I had to hang on to in all this hell."

"But these are gods!"

"I don't know what they are, but gods they are not."

"Evil is what they are!" Calandra interjected. "I have seen too many fall to this blackness not to know what they are. Don't embrace them, sweet Indy. Not everything fantastical is healthy."

"And that is why you are on a leash, Mr Austerley," said Havers. "My leash. You seem to have an inordinate attraction to these matters. Miskatonic University at one point, I believe. Professor of Occultic Affairs. Kept in the background though. You never published much. Well, not openly. But the private material made interesting reading. And a copy of the book! You scare me, Mr Austerley. Curiosity killed the cat and unfortunately it may also flatten the house this time too. Yet you have such knowledge I cannot find anywhere else, and so you are on my leash. Don't make me pull it tight."

Austerley supped on his mild with disdain. Also looking deep into his pint was Kirkgordon, musing on the situation. After some thirty seconds of uncomfortable silence, Havers interrupted his thoughts.

"What is it, Mr Kirkgordon?"

"Nothing. We really have nothing. We don't know what except that it's going to be big..."

"Cyclopean!"

"Shush, Indy. We don't know where, either. All we have is a delivery address for a small piece of the puzzle. Where was the buyer going to send the package, Havers?"

"The plan was to take it to another town and from there post it, in the normal post, to a Scottish island off the West Coast. The island only has about a hundred people living on it. But that is where we are heading, once you sup up. There's a Hercules awaiting us out on one of the pans."

"Are we going covert or overt?"

"Overt I think, Mr Kirkgordon. I doubt Mr Austerley could be covert. We'll pick up some essentials in Scotland when we land. It will be a boat to the island and a small one too, I believe. We'll go armed. Never know what we will find."

"No pistols, Havers. Unwise around Indy. Trust me."

"As you suggest, Mr Kirkgordon, just a small side arm for myself in case of emergencies."

Havers looked at his team. A haggard, recently beaten Elder junkie scared of guns. A broken-down former protection agent with serious marriage issues. And an extremely old woman whose leg seems to be falling apart. Oh well, he thought, I hear the fishing's good.

Chapter 16

An Island Welcome

"Is he always so quiet?"

"No, Mr Havers. Not always." Kirkgordon had started addressing Havers as a Mister, deliberately ignoring his Major. Never having been a military man, he had a distrust of uniformed people and, despite working with many over the course of his former career, he had never fully accepted the notion that anyone was in complete charge.

"What's he doing?"

"Crouching on the end of a boat staring into the depths of the sea."

"There's no requirement to be facetious. Calandra, what is he doing?"

Calandra, now dressed in tight blue jeans and a

red crop top, over which sat a black leather jacket, turned round to face the pair. Kirkgordon could have sworn she was going to a rock concert, not a potential hellhole, and the knee-length black boots just encouraged these thoughts. She's so like Alana. Aside from the extremely pale complexion, of course.

"He's checking the deep," said Calandra, "looking for any signs of disturbance. So far I haven't seen anything. But this fog isn't helping. I'm surprised auld Jim is capable of piloting this anywhere. There's maybe twenty feet of distance. At least it's calm. Looks like your tabs weren't required, tough guy."

Constant little digs, thought Kirkgordon. Little barbs about everything. Probably deserve it, though, for that comment in the mess. Damn. At least I'm getting something from her. Austerley's gone so quiet since Havers called him out. He's like a brooding vulture awaiting some poor bugger's death.

"I'll take my tabs all the same. Little bit eerie though, isn't it?"

"In what way? What are you seeing, Mr Kirkgordon?"

"Hearing, not seeing. Or rather not hearing. Seagulls, where are they? I grew up on the coast and I don't know any without some sort of bird life, fog or no fog. They would tail the boats looking for food."

"When we left there were some. I know, cos one nearly crapped on my jacket."

"Yeah, Calandra, and now listen... nothing except the lap of the water. No porpoise or dolphin or even a seal on the way over. That's not uncommon, but combined with the total lack of gulls... something isn't right. Austerley?"

"What?" Austerley spat back at him.

"Seagulls?"

"Stopped about ten minutes ago. Haven't seen a fish either. Deadest water I've ever seen."

"Oi! Jim! How far are we from shore?"

"Reckon a good ten minutes," said the boat's captain. "Hard to tell in this fog but that's what the GPS says."

"We will keep to our 'visiting tourists' plan," said Havers. "How could we have known there were no birds? Should make a good question. Oh, and Mr Kirkgordon, what is that extra case of yours?" The case in question was narrow but long and flat in the third dimension. It had the look of a tough shell exterior.

"You advised weaponry, Mr Havers. So weaponry I have brought."

"You were unable to find something smaller? Like my little Glock?"

"Austerley doesn't like guns. Trust me, they make him freak. He becomes unpredictable and generally even more chaotic. Arrows don't make the same sort of noise."

"Ah, I see. I shall refrain until necessary."

"Always a good maxim."

"The best weapon," Calandra interrupted, "sits in plain sight." Leaning on her staff, she smiled and touched her lame leg knowingly.

"Is that a light up ahead?"

"Damn, your eyes are good, Churchy."

Kirkgordon didn't tell Calandra that he had seen the light just over her shoulder while casting an indulgent survey of her body. Oh God, help me focus.

"Time to make our entrance, so everyone look sharp, and look like a tourist. Oh, and Mr Kirkgordon," Havers dropped to a whisper, "keep a damn good eye on Mr Austerley. He looks somewhat compromised to me." Compromised! He had been in that damned institution for a reason.

Apart from the gentle lapping of the water on the boat's edge, there was only the gentle putt-putt of the engine. Gradually, a stone harbour wall could be made out, and the boat's skipper gently steered alongside. Kirkgordon leapt up onto the pier's edge and fastened a rope to the buttress. Reaching down to a smiling Calandra, he pulled her up, whereupon she hobbled until Austerley threw her staff to her.

"Straight back, skipper, then wait a maximum of two days. If you haven't heard anything from us then it's a full go for an island invasion." The boat's captain doffed his cap then threw some of the bags onto the quayside.

"Good luck, Major. See you soon." With Austerley and Havers both on shore, the skipper calmly reversed the little boat and disappeared slowly into the gloom.

"Very little light considering we should be at the main harbour. Not a damn beacon or anything."

Havers scoured the area around him for any sign of life.

"Mr Havers," whispered Kirkgordon, "your three o'clock, behind the wall. And that's just the first one."

"Hmm. Well, let's make our acquaintance. You, behind the wall, where's the nearest lodging? Here for a spot of bird watching. Possibly not tonight, blighters seem damn quiet. So where's the nearest hostel, my good man?"

Austerley had wandered off to a spot on the quayside. Staring intently at a signpost, he was nearly left behind by the others, who were making their way to the local. Calandra was the first to see him dallying and strode back over.

"What is it?" A hand dropped onto Austerley's shoulder, immediately breaking his mood and defences. She knew him too well.

"The names on the signpost," he answered, enjoying the rubbing of a tight knot, "seem familiar."

"Federal Place, Washington Avenue, La Fayette. Not very island to me."

"No," agreed Austerley, "not Gaelic, or even Scots. Not Norse either. But definitely familiar. Just can't place them at the moment."

"Cally, Austerley, get over here, this man's going to show us to the local. Apparently they've got real ale on tap. Local stuff."

"Hear that, Indy? Proper beer. Maybe this place won't be so bad."

Austerley just murmured under his breath and

slowly turned to follow, laboriously picking up his khaki holdall. Calandra walked quickly but awkwardly to join alongside Kirkgordon, her leg still suffering from Farthington's attentions.

"Might be a small place, Churchy. Hope you don't mind sharing!"

She's a damn tease, thought Kirkgordon. But she knows how to. And she knows I like it.

It was only a five hundred yard walk along a gravel path before the first building came into sight. Their guide had said nothing, merely employing grunts and arm-pointing when needed. Despite being young, he was obviously balding, and clearly staring at Calandra with somewhat bulbous eyes.

"It would appear our Sherpa has a taste for paler women, Mr Austerley," said Havers.

"Humph. Possibly."

"Come now. Personal feelings aside, please. We are all going to need to get along on this spotter's holiday." Austerley glared at the guide watching Calandra and his hands flexed into fists.

The first building was a house of two storeys built in that drab pebbledash so abundant in Scotland. No lights were on, but Kirkgordon swore he saw movement inside. Soon they were in the middle of a village street with houses on either side and then a pub appeared out of the night with a single shining light outside. The guide went up to the rather decrepit door and banged on it three times. Austerley looked up at the legend on the front of the building. In rather brash and jaunty writing was the single word "Elliot's".

"So, where are we?" Austerley interrogated the unsuspecting guide. He looked back blankly, staring like a fish in a bowl. "This street? What's its name?"

"We're in Scotland, Indy. No need to speak to them like foreigners." Kirkgordon shook his head.

"New Church Green. Church is over there. And there's the green. That's why we call it that." The voice was almost a croak. It seemed the vocal chords hadn't been designed for speech and the noise that came out bore no recognizable accent. The door opened.

"Yes?" This voice was dull and dry, but more human.

"Ah, my good man. We got into a bit of a late start getting here, then the boat lost an engine, so we're a bit late. Would you have any accommodation for our little party? Just a night or two, I believe. Twitchers, you see. Bit of bird watching."

"One room only. One double bed, one single bed. Shower's broke. No breakfast. Out of season."

"O...kay, I'm sure we will manage. Can we get any food tonight? Or a drink?"

"Bar's closed 'til nine. Everyone's been at church. Open at nine. Thirty pounds for the room."

"Okay. That will do, my good man. Lead the way."

"Straight through to the stairs. Third floor. Last room. Only one open. Nine o'clock." And with that the man let the door close. Havers pushed it back open quickly and watched the man turn to enter a side room. The guide, too, had walked off.

"Oh well, better check the room, everyone."

"Warm welcome!" laughed Calandra.

"Come on," said Kirkgordon. "Next time, Havers, I'll book the accommodation. You coming, Indy?" Austerley was once again staring at the "Elliot's" sign at the building's front. Slowly he bowed his head and picked up his bag to follow.

"Church? On a Tuesday night? Never known that. And I've been round most denominations," Kirkgordon remarked.

"Well," said Havers, "the Scottish islands are known for the religious spirit. Oh, and the alcohol!"

They squeezed their way up some narrow wooden stairs before reaching the landing on the third floor. Kirkgordon tried all the doors on the floor but, as the landlord had stated, only the last was open.

"Well friends, it's a tad tight!" Kirkgordon laughed, before being shunted further into the room by Austerley.

"Been in smaller. For the last five years, actually."

"Ah! Now, this could be awkward. I suggest Miss Calandra takes the single bed and the gentlemen share the double. Best to have someone on watch through the night anyway."

There was barely standing room for the four colleagues, and they shuffled and fussed around each other until Austerley stormed out of the room announcing he was going for a cigarette. From the doorway, the double bed was located on the left side of the room with the single on the other. A narrow strip of bare brown carpet was the only gap, forcing their bags to be loaded on top of each other at the end of the double bed. Underneath each bed a crude wooden barrier prevented any storage.

"I think I'll take the air like Mr Austerley. The room's extremely fusty."

As soon as Havers closed the door behind him, Calandra sat down on the single bed, lifting her leg in a painful fashion to stretch it out.

"You okay, Churchy?"

"No."

"Am I too forward?"

"No... well, yes."

"Sorry."

"It's not you, Cally... well, it is but it's not. Arse, I'm not putting this well." Kirkgordon sat on the double bed and studied Calandra's face. She looked a little hurt but more confused than anything else.

"Havers got my family out. He was worried they would be targeted. So he took them away. The kids and Alana. And back at the auction I got to speak to her. Cally, she's been with me for so long. She gave me kids and then, when all this crap with Austerley and the graveyard kicked off, well, it near broke her. Broke us. I was wild at times. Some nights I even thrashed out. I was just falling apart. A wreck. But a brutal one. Especially in my dreams."

"You hit her?"

"Yes. Not deliberately, during a nightmare. Cally, I broke her jaw."

"But it wasn't your fault. You were

compromised."

"It wasn't a mission. She wasn't a protectee or a target, or even a bystander. She was mine. And I hurt her. We had to part. We didn't speak. I saw the kids next to never."

"I'm sorry. I thought you were... available."

"It's not your fault. Damn it, it's not like I look the other way. But on the phone at the auction, she called me C. She was my wife again. My woman. My Alana. Do you understand?"

"Yes." Calandra looked at the ceiling, inhaled deeply, and braced herself for the attacks from her mind, which was screaming that she had lost.

"Cally, you're really not cold at all."

"No. Just very lonely."

He kissed her forehead. "Sorry. You deserve more."

"I'm just out of my time." Calandra smiled. "But I'll take a pint."

Chapter 17

Elliot's Bar

Walking into the bar area of "Elliot's", Kirkgordon was slightly bemused. The assumption that many heads would turn and check out Calandra, a draw even out of her black leathers, was an obvious one. Instead, from the mainly male clientele, there was little of that sex's usual animal instinct at all. But they watched. Or, rather, stared intently, like they had no shame, or any understanding of shame. And it wasn't just Calandra but also Kirkgordon they were interested in.

"Did I just walk into a gentleman's club or something?"

"Not one like I've been in."

"So you frequent those places?""

"Enough! What you having?""

Kirkgordon wasn't sure the barman would know a good Rioja if it was spilt on him but that was what the lady wanted. On leaving the upstairs room, the tension between them had turned into a false dawn of buddies together. Part of him wanted to get as far away from her as possible, but another appreciated the womanly presence. At least this was a better way of working; he needed to focus.

The same man who had answered the door glared at Kirkgordon from behind the bar. Calmly pushing his way to the bar's edge, Kirkgordon tried to ignore the eyes of the man sat on the stool beside him, which had the look of two table-tennis balls placed under some straining pressure by an internal air pump, rather similar to a boiled egg just before it's apportioned by the slicer. Despite this distraction, Kirkgordon was able to say, "Pint of what's good and a Rioja for the lady. Decent glass too."

"No wine. Dark for yourself." Had this man missed out on the conversational barman course at training college?

"Mild for my friend, in that case." As the barman retreated to the glassware, Kirkgordon took in the state of the room that evening. Tables were sat back from the bar, ornate wooden affairs with matching chairs, many in need of repair. Screws were coming loose and joints creaked when their occupants moved even slightly. The bar front was full, with many sitting on high stools. On the walls were occasional pictures of fishing boats and large catches, which broke up the drab pale green paint, peeling with damp in many places. The buzz of a bar in late evening was absent, leaving only the extremely quiet, hushed conversations and glaring eyes. Kirkgordon reacted to this awkward situation head on.

"Now then, sir, how are you today?" The ping-pong-eyed man beside him said nothing. "Rather rough bit of fog on the way in, I doubt we'll get much twitching done 'til it's gone."

A face that could out-stare a military roadblock held its gaze steady. A few others turned to reinforce the barriers.

"Have you ever been much of a twitcher yourself?" Kirkgordon continued to talk to the air. "Sea birds up here, I guess. I mean, look at the photos on the wall." The man didn't look. "You must get all sorts of gulls hanging on the back of those. My dear old uncle Silas used to have a dredger. He was forever complaining about the 'damnable' seagulls always crapping on him at the back of the boat. He would have taken a rifle to them just for fun. Got him in the end though. Slipped on a piece of the boat deck and disappeared off starboard never to be seen again. Shocking!"

The least shocked visage in the world blanked back at Kirkgordon. Like two gunfighters at a corral, they fixed on each other until the sound of glasses on the bar top turned Kirkgordon's head. At the same time the pub door opened and Havers marched in, followed by a sauntering Austerley.

"Ah, Austerley. Just getting these drinks back to Cally but got the man here for you. Just fascinated by old fishing stories. Told him you'd have a few. Oh, and order Havers a mild while you're up there."

The seething eyes of hell raged out from under Austerley's brow but he took to his task.

"Two mild, my good man! Now then, tales of the sea, eh? Well, did you ever hear about the Kaponica sailing out of Dover to Port Elizabeth? No? Ah, your sort of story I think..."

Chuckling to himself, Kirkgordon sat down beside Calandra, opposite Havers. Amidst the dull greens and greys of the locals' clothing, Havers' bright blue wild-weather jacket was a positive beacon of fashion and practicality.

"Where's my wine?"

"Not sure this is your sort of high-class establishment. Not your level of elocution. Electrocution would be better, force them into speaking."

"Certainly, this area didn't receive the beauty gene," noted Havers. He glanced around. "How many bald people have you ever seen in a bar together?"

"You're right. I normally find them quite sexy, too," Calandra said, "but it's truly not happening here. Most of them look how you'd imagine the dirty mac brigade. And there's that smell."

"Yes," said Havers, "I thought it was the bar itself with the damp. The closer you get, the worse it becomes."

"And the beer's pish!" Kirkgordon complained.

"It doesn't seem to be stopping them, though. They're certainly game with it. That man on the right has had two pints since I came in the door. They drink like fish."

Austerley came to the table carrying two pints of mild, one half-consumed, and sat beside Havers.

"You okay, Indy?" asked Calandra. "You seem mighty agitated."

"We need to go!"

"Sorry?" said Havers.

"We need to go. Now!" came the half-whispered reply.

"Why? What's the matter?"

"This is not a place to stay. Elliot's. New Church Green. Drinking. Look at the hands. Look at the hands. Look!"

"Well, certainly no bass guitarists, but that's hardly a crime."

"Waites mild. Waites dark. Federal whisky. All made here, from here. What size shoes do you take? Do your gloves fit?"

"Calm down, Austerley. You're attracting attention. Calm down."

The door of the bar was flung open and a man in a colourful robe entered. Austerley stared hard at the balding middle-aged man then turned to Havers and delivered in a forced half-whisper, "E-O-D!"

And with that, Austerley collapsed.

Calandra was on her feet swiftly and caught him before he could slide off the chair, but even the chilling touch of her hands could not revive him.

She turned to see a looming figure.

"Not from round here, are ye?" The colourful robe led up to the face of a groundsman. Calandra felt as if she'd been caught on the grass next to an abundance of signs forbidding it. "Difficult place to understand, strange weather. Best not make it a long trip." Having delivered his warning, the man turned away to the door. All was silent in the pub and all eyes were focused on the table where Austerley lay slumped. Havers stepped up to face the local pressure.

"A glass of water, my good man. Yes, you! Behind the bar, you! My friend needs some water if you would be so good as to oblige. Thank you, sir, most kind."

Since the man in the coloured robe had walked in, Kirkgordon had gone to high alert, constantly assessing the room. His old days as protection detail came in useful and an escape plan was starting to form. He doubted any of the men in the bar could match Calandra or himself, but Austerley's incapacitation was a negative factor in their safety. He had also spotted a logo on the robed man which displayed the same letters that had featured in Austerley's collapse: EOD.

The water arrived in a filthy glass and appeared cloudy. Havers took one look at it, decided it would be better for Austerley's health to keep the water on the outside and chucked the entire glassful over his face. Austerley murmured slightly but remained slumped.

"Okay," whispered Havers, "time, I think, to

leave. Mr Kirkgordon, can you carry him?" Kirkgordon nodded. "Right then, we'll retire upstairs and discuss our options there. It certainly seems we are unwelcome here."

Kirkgordon went to his knees and then rolled Austerley over his shoulder, muttering the words "fat git" under his breath. The bar remained silent while the whole party retreated to their room. Havers had to exit the bedroom to allow Kirkgordon space to enter and dump Austerley, in unceremonious fashion, onto the larger bed. Once everyone had found a space in the room, Kirkgordon sat down, leaning against the now-shut entrance.

"E-O-D! E-O-D! They're coming! Rising up from the deep! Elder coming! Mother Hydra! Mother Hydra! All here to praise! Call him forth!"

"Shut up, Austerley!"

"Don't be so harsh, Churchy," Calandra scolded. "My Count, dearest Count, are you there? Listen, my love, hush the voices, listen to me, my voice." For a moment Austerley seemed to quieten down, but suddenly he lashed out with his arms as he delivered the next torrent, sending Calandra sprawling backwards.

"Mother Hydra! No, no, no, no. Where's the hope? Where to hide? E-O-D! E-O-D! Moth..."

"Mr Kirkgordon, silence him!" It almost sounded like a kill order, thought Kirkgordon. Regardless, he stepped forward and jabbed hard in the region of Austerley's neck. Austerley collapsed and caught his head against the wall. The remaining three sat in silence for the next minute.

"It seems we have a slight issue," said Havers, master of the understatement. "I believe Mr Austerley has a good idea of what we are dealing with, but his mind is in a somewhat fluctuating state. Given the possibility of time not being on our side, I suggest, Mr Kirkgordon, that you go on a little wander and see what you can dig up. Take Miss Calandra with you, see what secrets you can find. The church may be worth a little perusal. I'll stay with our friend and keep him quiet."

"Are you sure that's wise, Mr Havers? The locals don't seem happy to see us. If you need to move quickly are you sure you can carry Austerley?"

"Don't worry about Havers, Churchy. You don't get to his position if you can't handle yourself. Time to blacken up."

"Okay, but Havers?"

"Yes?"

"Back of the neck like I just did. It's an easy spot. Should quieten him down if he gets frisky."

"Mr Kirkgordon, I think I can find infinitely better spots to strike, certainly less crude."

"Ooh, touché!" laughed Calandra.

She reached into her canvas bag and produced a black leather jacket, black leggings, a black belt and a dark grey crop top. Without a moment's hesitation she stripped down to her underwear before dressing back up. She tied up her hair, looking at Kirkgordon before muttering something about it being a good job they were all professionals. As he dressed in his covert outfit, again mainly black, Kirkgordon agreed, but standing in his pants and socks he somehow didn't cut the same "professional" figure.

Calandra smeared her face in black paint then handed the container to Kirkgordon. They couldn't hear much noise coming from downstairs but neither had they heard many people leaving. He glanced out of the small window on the far side of the room. It was fixed on two hinges and seemed to be able to swing completely open with only one handle latch keeping it closed.

"Best take the window, Cally." Calandra nodded.

"Havers, we'll be no more than four hours." Kirkgordon said. "We'll tap your name in Morse on the window to get back in. There's a gutter just at the side, old but looks like it will hold."

"Four hours, Mr Kirkgordon. Find me something!"

"That sounds like an order."

"Four hours, Mr Kirkgordon. Don't make me come and look for you."

Calandra gently opened the window and swung nimbly onto the guttering. Her leg was clearly bothering her but she seemed capable of ignoring the pain. Once she had reached the ground, Kirkgordon threw down her staff. He took the quiver from its oddly shaped case and strapped it on, then secured the bow across his chest. After one last look at a slumbering Austerley, he jumped on to the sill before sailing down the gutter. Glancing down, Calandra was almost invisible in the dark.

"Is Havers really that good?"

"Trust me, Austerley's in good hands."

"I hope so. After everything, I still feel sorry for the stupid arse."

"Heads up, local five hundred metres ahead."

"I'm on point. Let's go!"

Chapter 18

A New Denomination

Holding to the shadows in the village was an easy process. Most of the street lights gave out a dim orange glow as if the bulbs were toward the end of their lives. Where the light did fall, there were plenty of jutting corners and a myriad of small alleys to conceal oneself in. The night was cold with a waning moon and, although not a totally clear sky, it was sparse enough to allow for a light frosting on the ground.

"Possibility of snow," whispered Calandra. She was crouched at the side of a small house staring at the church across the green. There were a few locals hanging around a nearby streetlamp clutching small brown paper bags with the tops of bottles sticking out. Conversation amongst them was practically non-existent, the occasional muttering sounding an air of complaint.

"If we circuit quickly to the east side we should be able to get past them and jump inside the church wall." An uneasy feeling was rising in Kirkgordon. He tried to ignore the images which kept returning to him: the face of the robed man in the pub, Austerley's chaotic behaviour. It was in the graveyard last time. That was the last time Austerley had flipped this badly. An imposing fear growing at the front of his mind was proving difficult to be dispassionate about.

The church had a classical stone wall surrounding it, with a further walled area behind it containing many gravestones. The greyish building was bland on the outside with a small noticeboard located beside its front door.

No one saw the two black figures throw themselves over the five foot high wall and land with little noise on the grass behind. Silently, they performed a half-crouch, half-walk to the wooden double door at the front of the church.

"Entwined Order of Divinity? Members only? We don't have that in Europe. Is that a Scottish or British denomination?" wondered Calandra aloud, reading the board on the wall.

"Never heard of it. But the initials. EOD. That's what Austerley was raving about. Doesn't look abnormal from the outside. We need to get inside. Can you pick a lock?"

"No. But as it's open, it shouldn't matter."

Opening the right-hand door ever so slowly to prevent it from creaking, Calandra entered. Kirkgordon followed close behind and gently closed the entrance. Inside was dark, but it revealed itself as their eyes slowly adjusted, like peering into a fog. There was one single room with chairs laid out like a traditional nave with a pulpit set off to the front right-hand side. On the far wall, facing the chairs, was a large motif incorporating a multi-headed creature standing with a hideous dark winged being. Even from this distance the letters EOD were obvious.

"Let's see what we can find. See the pictures on the walls? You take them. I'll see if there's anything amongst the chairs and then take a look at the motif." Calandra headed off toward the pictures, ignoring the obvious damp pervading each wall. Kirkgordon quickly inspected the seats, looking for anything that might give a clue to the activities of the Entwined Order of Divinity.

The chairs seemed precarious to sit on, many in a severely rotted state, far from their days of mahogany glory. Kirkgordon wondered if any of the townsfolk could actually sit on them. As he approached the front, he sneaked a quick glance at Calandra examining various portraits on the wall. Alana had looked good in leggings too, he thought, especially with a ponytail dropping down, her delicate ears bared. The deft line of her neck was also very enticing. Focus, dammit, focus.

Suddenly there was a glint from the front of the room. There, in front of the chairs, was a long table supporting several objects. From his current distance they were indistinct, but the glint had come from the left-hand side. Creeping forward, Kirkgordon saw the flash of light again. Moonlight was glimmering through an upper skylight and catching the studded jewels on the piece on the left. Getting closer, Kirkgordon soon identified a crown of some sort. Alongside it was a colourful robe, draped over the table, plus a small safe box and a large envelope.

"Churchy, over here!" came the whispered request.

Kirkgordon's mind lingered on the crown, reason beating against his brain but with the door still firmly shut. Confused, he acceded to Calandra's request. She was looking intently at a portrait of some kind of amphibian. The animal had long spindly legs with distinctly frog-like webbed feet. It wore a grey duffel coat over its large body. The head was a horrific combination of human and frog. The jawline was jutting and taut like a fit human male but the eyes were bulbous with massive black irises. A few remnants of silvery hair donned the edges of the face but up top was a slippery green surface.

"A Pickman?"

"No! No. Definitely not."

"Why, Calandra? Why are you sure?" Kirkgordon stared at the picture, struggling to take in the abomination presented. When he turned to Calandra for an answer he saw her shaking. Not the panic of a frightened deer but rather the realization of a scholar who sees the damage wrought by years of work. He touched her shoulder and she turned, burying her face into the warmth of his body. Lifting her chin, he stared deep into her frightened eyes and tried to provide reassurance and hope. But she just stared back.

"Cally, what? If it's not a Pickman, then what? Whose is it?"

"I don't... I don't... Hell, I don't know!"

"Shush, Cally, shush! They'll hear you. I don't understand. What's to fear from a picture?"

"It's a portrait! Don't you get it? It's a portrait!"

"Okay, okay. It's a portrait. Like Pickman, live models, real things. But it's from another place, another time. Why the fear?"

"Look! Dammit, look, Churchy." Calandra pointed at the picture. "Recognize the church on the green behind it? The house just along, that tree?"

"It's from here. But that doesn't mean it's from now."

"The buildings match up perfectly. The season is right. And that is not painted with the paint of the Pickman years. Churchy, do you see? That's modern paint! I'd say that picture is less than a month old!"

And the creatures from the graveyard came back at him. In they came, occasionally slowed by his guns. Whipping arms and fists around him, slashing his back and sides. He was fighting back with one arm and both legs as best he could, grabbing Austerley by the collar with the other hand. Closing his eyes, Kirkgordon forced his breathing into a measured pulse: in, then out. His ears took in the silence. His body felt Calandra tremble. His nose suddenly picked up the slightest of fishy odours. Pulse slowing. On opening his eyes, his state was calm but a strong shiver of dread raced down his back.

"Okay, Cally. Ease up. Breathe. We're alone at the moment, nothing to fear here." She clung on for a moment before stepping back and drawing herself up. However, her wetted eyes were obvious. She's fearless before dragons, thought Kirkgordon, so what hell are we into now?

"Is there anything in any of the other pictures?" he asked.

"They're older, mainly. The last one is the most fearful. A Shuggoth. Fallen servant of the Eldars. Uncontrollable now. That picture is at least three hundred years old, thank goodness. There's a hydra there too. Indy mentioned a hydra."

"Yes, Mother Hydra." They stood and stared for a moment, lost in horrific contemplation.

"Cally, come look at this." Kirkgordon led the way over to the table and gently lifted up the crown. "Ever seen a crown like this?"

"Technically, it's a tiara, Churchy. New one on me though." Calandra, seeing that it was obviously too small for Kirkgordon's head, tried to delicately place it on her own. For a good minute she tried to get the item to fit but was unable. It would slide first at one side and then the other but never both at once.

"Guess I'm just too big for it."

"No, Cally, look at it! The shape. It's not round, it's like... squashed in. Stretched out."

"Elliptical?"

"Yeah, that one."

"And it's supposed to be your language."

"What fits that shape?"

"Not what, Churchy. Who! Possibly something amphibian?"

"Froggy?"

"Possibly, or maybe fishy?"

Kirkgordon shuddered. "Fish are not amphibians."

"And frogs don't combine with humans, I suppose? Churchy, there are things in the ocean your trawlers don't want to catch!"

"What's in the envelope?" Cally asked.

Taking it in trembling hands, Kirkgordon reached inside the already open envelope and pulled out a familiar-looking manuscript. "It's Zahn's music. From half the world away to here. Not even a scorch mark on it!"

"At least we can hold on to that. Or maybe we should burn it. Then they would have to go and fetch it again."

"Nice idea, Cally, but look at this. It's not the original, it's a photocopy. A good one. The colour, the quality, but it's definitely a copy. Not a lot of point getting rid of it."

"Still, pocket it, Churchy."

"Cally, look at the table. Do you see the dust?"

"What's so strange about that? The whole place

is decayed and damp. There's dust just about everywhere you look."

"Except for there. Look at that!" On the table was a small, fairly round patch of clean table. The edges of the circle were slightly uneven. "That looks like the imprint of a soft bag, Cally. There's been something else here. Something important, I guess. I wonder..."

"What? You look worried."

"Well, yeah, but I've been worried ever since we came into this building. But, Cally, why keep all these items together? It's like a collection. But now some are gone. No original manuscript. A missing bag. Is something on the move? Remember what Austerley said. Frog-men on the prowl, too."

"Time to get Havers, Churchy. He'll storm the place with this sort of evidence. Especially that frog-man. Time for backup. He's got a radio to call the boatman back in. Time to go." Calandra stared hard, waiting for Kirkgordon's response.

"Yeah," said Kirkgordon scanning around slowly, making sure they had looked at everything. "Time to go."

Chapter 19

The Way of the Frog

"That thing is hopping, Churchy!"

It may have been a forced whisper but it still chilled Kirkgordon to his core. Despite his recent contemplation of the picture in the church, the actual reality of a frog-man was shaking his mind. Granted, this image, approximately one hundred yards away, was less graphic due to the robe and hood that covered most of the figure, but the motion beneath was beyond all natural sense.

"Don't, Cally! Focus, breathe. Havers is the point. Two corners and we're there."

I'm out of my depth here, thought Kirkgordon. She fought a dragon, she's four hundred years old or something, she disappears into the ground and reappears countries away, and yet she's petrified. Tiaras, music, frog-men and a raving lunatic to get clear of it all. Thank goodness Havers is a professional. At least Alana's okay. So think, breathe. Get Havers, Austerley. Radio the boat and get out! Let the military blow this fiasco sky high.

"Okay, it's clear. I'll go first. See you at the corner, Cally." Swiftly but gracefully, the two figures glided across cold streets back to the inn where they had left their colleagues. Upon reaching the last corner, Kirkgordon dropped to a knee, raising a hand indicating "stop" to Calandra behind him. A small crowd was gathered at the bottom of the gutter from which the black-clad pair had descended just a few hours ago. Some of the gathering Kirkgordon recognized from the bar, but several figures defied belief. Humanoid figures with distinctly fish-like markings confirmed Calandra's earlier suspicions. Gills and fins adorned several creatures. One had scales running down his naked torso, overlaid on a mostly human pair of shoulders. Another lacked ears but sported a pronounced set of eyes. Hideous likenesses of this pair were voicing their concern about a smashed window on the side of the pub. He noticed the voices were not all human, some were just croaks and bubbling noises. The natural human voice had been tainted by, presumably, altered vocal chords.

Doubling back, Kirkgordon found Calandra behind a hedge. Given her recent candour, he was debating how much to tell her.

"There's a crowd there. I have no idea what's

happened," said Kirkgordon, deciding on honesty as the best solution.

"They'll be okay. They will. Havers is good. Real good. Best I have seen. Okay? They'll be okay. Won't they?"

"Calandra, we have to go. We need to leave. This is getting too big. Can you make an exit? Like in Russia?"

"Yes. You're right. Exit. Just wait and I'll do it. Right here. Yes." She drew with a shaking hand but within a minute she had placed a chalk outline on the ground.

"Okay, Cally. Let's go." They stepped into the markings together and waited. But there was nothing. Kirkgordon thought Calandra's face turned even whiter.

"What's up? What's wrong, Cally?"

"Evil. I'm sorry. The evil. It's blocking it. We're stuck here."

"Can't you, like, zap it, or get past it? Do you know where it's coming from?"

Calandra shook her head. "Churchy, don't you get it? It's the place, the time, everything. These are deeper powers from ages past. This is an evil beyond what you know. The whole place. This is like your worst legends coming back. Shuggoth. There was a picture of a Shuggoth. You don't just fight those things. We're up to our necks in it."

"Not if I can help it. Time to find another exit. Stay close, Cally." Kirkgordon hoped his little speech had looked like a Hollywood moment because now, with his face turned, the terror of

Calandra's failure was hitting home. Time to start moving before the panic took him.

As they silently moved away from the main streets, back out towards the harbour, snow in light puffs of white drifted to the ground. Sod it, thought Kirkgordon, it's cold enough for it to lie. Another hour or so and we'll be easily traceable.

Arriving back at the harbour everything looked calm and peaceful. The previous fog was sitting a little off the shore. The Christmas-card harbour wharf was starting to change from its usual dirty yellow to a clean white, but that did little to remove the air of decay. Instead, the snow just fell on broken pieces of pallets, creels and netting.

The pair crouched and observed for some five minutes before feeling secure enough to race down to the wharf, looking for a small tied-up boat. Kirkgordon remembered at least one when they landed, but now, none.

"Okay, so that's a non-starter. We'll need to scour the shorelines and check for any others. Certainly no sign of Indy and Havers round here. I'd say this place is deserted. Not surprising as there were a lot of them around the pub there. What do you think, Cally? Cally, I said what do you think?"

"Shush!" Kirkgordon followed Cally's eyes down into the water. Nothing, he could see nothing.

He tapped her shoulder but she wouldn't turn to him so he moved to stand in front of her face. "What?" he mouthed.

"Frog-man," came the silent response.

Crescendo!

Nonchalantly, so as not to show his awareness, Kirkgordon turned to the water and could just make out two dark bulbous eyes lurking in the water. And then they moved.

Sea water sprayed high as the creature sprang up. Its feet were webbed and attached to long, spindly yet amazingly powerful legs, judging by the distance covered. The legs contorted into massive human hips but the flesh was moist and slimy. The torso sported a ribcage but the arms were thin and green. The head was definitively frog-like except for the bared teeth. They were decayed, and a pale yellow, but most definitely human. But the most dangerous item was the trident on a metal shaft that the creature was attempting to bring down with force onto Kirkgordon's head.

Calandra's warning had been enough and Kirkgordon rolled hard to his right before standing tall again. His bow was off his shoulder and an arrow mounted just shy of the frog-man's second leap. This time his target was Calandra but she rebuffed him with her twirling staff, ends blazing in white light. Following up, she struck the creature on the hip. It barely seemed to notice and countered with a slash of its trident, cutting across her face. She reeled and tripped backwards, dropping her staff. The creature leapt into the air, turning its trident in order to land on Calandra and drive its barbs straight through her chest. An arrow, reaching its apex, drove deep into one of its enormous eyes, followed by a second arrow burying into the other eye. A deafening croak rang through the air and the creature somehow managed to land on its webbed feet. Rising, Calandra grabbed her staff and swung it hard into the neck of the amphibian, breaking all connections. Its feet whipped upwards, the head spun down into the ground and a limp corpse lay motionless, to be gently covered by the increasingly heavy snow.

"Are you okay?" Kirkgordon hurried over to Calandra.

"Yeah, it's sore but it's just a cut." Kirkgordon looked closely at Cally's pale face which now had two moderate gorges of red. It should have been flowing with her blood but instead it seemed some miniature wall of ice was holding it back.

"The joy of being a chilled-out girl, I guess. Thanks, Churchy."

"There's no boat here and that scream's gonna bring them running. We need to move, Cally. You okay?"

"The knee's sore. It'll be a hobble." She looked deeply into his worried face. "Leave me."

"Like hell." Kirkgordon dropped his shoulder, grabbed her round the back of the knees and lifted her up and over. He surveyed the scene ahead. There was a path through some thick gorse, narrow, possibly a sheep path. Try and get webbed feet through that, he thought.

A glint from the frog-man's neck caught his eye. Carefully, Kirkgordon bent down beside it with Cally still draped over his shoulder. A chain, heavily tarnished, was catching a nearby light. He quickly snapped the chain from the creature's neck and gave it a cursory examination. It carried a pendant which displayed a large winged creature with the letters EOD beneath it. Like we needed another denomination, thought Kirkgordon, throwing the pendant away.

A quick glance over his shoulder showed lights coming from the main village. Time to run again. I thought I'd given all this nonsense up. He ran hard towards the gorse. His shoulder felt the chill from Calandra's body, which had nestled in. Austerley was just a freak show to Alana. Cally would be a bit more difficult to explain. But Austerley was missing, Havers too, and he didn't have a clue how any of this worked. His survival instincts were running a stopwatch, timing his would-be pursuers from the village. His interior alarms were sounding loudly, so he clutched Cally tight and scuttled off into the gorse.

Chapter 20

The House in the Snow

Snow is beautiful, covering all with its most perfect of blankets. Swirling and whirling, occasionally blinding, as we plough on to who knows where? I always get a little poetic on the run, thought Kirkgordon. Still, at least it's not Austerley over my shoulder.

A little guilt came over him as he wondered whether Austerley was lying in some dismembered state somewhere with a broken ex-civil servant. No matter how much anger he felt toward the "stupid arse", he could never feel the pure disdain that Alana had for him. That frog-man, though. The very idea of creatures like that. Hopping. Just hopping. It was comical in some senses, but the creature had moved so quickly and with such killing intent. And the "stupid arse" had prevented him from bringing guns.

Kirkgordon had deliberately tried to stay away from the shoreline since the frog-man's attack, but the gorse-lined track he was following had become so enclosed he had temporarily lost his bearings, and he now emerged suddenly onto the machair at the beach-side. Quickly, he scanned to see if there was anything sitting out in the open. His eyes were drawn to a figure on the beach, motionless and seemingly face down.

"Cally, I'm gonna drop you here."

"And your wife thought you were chivalrous? Nothing like protecting a lady."

"I'll drop you in that hollow over there. If you're in the gorse I can't get an arrow near you."

"Black doesn't seem a good choice anymore. Left my white ball gown at home, unfortunately."

"Are you going to be all right? It's pretty exposed and that wind's picking up. Don't want you freezing to death."

"Are you taking the piss?"

Kirkgordon smiled. She was damn likeable. He hurried quickly to the hollow and dropped Cally rather unceremoniously before racing down to the beach. The figure hadn't moved but was covered in a thin white veil of snow. Kirkgordon got close and touched the figure's neck. It was stone cold. He brushed snow off the figure's face and recognized the captain who had brought them over. At least, he remembered the hat, hair and stubble from his chin.

The rest of the face could only be described as having been devoured.

"Dear God. What is this? I mean it, God! What is this?"

God appeared silent on the matter and Kirkgordon felt a gut-wrenching hollow. Up until now, there had been almost an excitement behind his candour, complaining and swearing about the damn nuisance of it all, but this changed things. He hadn't taken Austerley and his warnings seriously enough. This was worse than the graveyard. He was beginning to believe this could be an evil apocalypse. No! He had to start thinking tactically and not emotionally.

Searching the deceased captain's pockets yielded nothing except copious amounts of seaweed, leading him to the theory that the killing had happened at sea. Yet the body had been dragged ashore – there were two long lines in the sand lightly covered with snow. Kirkgordon looked around but the only other marks were his own. Anyway, he thought, it's too open. Time to move on. Within a minute he had picked up Calandra again and was racing into some new gorse on the far side of the beach.

The snow was now falling heavily and the wind was throwing it around like a wrestling main event. Calandra was not the only one who was cold, and Kirkgordon knew that shelter was essential.

It was now obvious to Kirkgordon that he was following a circuitous route with regards to the island. At his current rate he would be back in the main village within two hours. In honesty, there was no plan, just a hope that something might crop up. He couldn't swim off the island. On land the frogmen were extremely agile and strong. In the water... he didn't want to think about it. The boat and Havers' captain were gone. And as for Havers and Austerley... no, he needed a break of some sort. Some way of communicating with the outside world would be good. There had been the occasional payphone in the village but the place was too hot to risk any public activity. There had been no mobile signal since they'd landed.

The game was afoot. Clearly life was expendable and no mercy could be expected. Calandra's most strange mode of transport was blocked. He wished for Austerley now. Indy was a master of these situations, how to undo evil spells, castings or whatever they were.

He stopped. Ahead was a small beach house, set just up from the shore. Fairly old, its wooden decor had a faded look even in the poor moonlight. At the front was a small balcony area with a set of steps. From the side he couldn't tell how many windows were there, but the height of the house indicated two floors and possibly four to five rooms at best.

"Did you see that?" Calandra was peering round from over his shoulder but was focused on a spot just in front of the house.

"No, what?"

"Light. Torch, small, pen-like. Very brief."

"And do you see the roof?"

"Radio aerial! Smart."

"We need to check it out. Just running won't do us any good. We need help."

"Agreed. If you can get me to the house side I can hobble behind you."

"Can you fly?"

"I'd rather not, but if I have to... When he threw me down, it felt like half my back broke. Flying's going to be sore." Calandra grimaced as she spoke.

"Okay. Just keep an eye behind me. We don't know if these things can sniff." Without hesitation, Kirkgordon raced quickly to the house side before gently dropping Calandra onto her feet. She winced but gave a thumbs up. With his bow drawn, Kirkgordon crept to the front edge of the house, only once checking on Calandra's progress.

The escape had worn him down, especially having carried Calandra for most of it. Constantly pushing back the thoughts of the horrors awaiting had taken its toll, too. But this tension, this anticipation of the next encounter, was sapping every last bit of strength. All that was keeping him going was a nervous energy which he neither trusted nor wanted. He breathed slowly and surely, trying to control his nerves and body.

It was there again. Very brief but bright. Circular and intense. Definitely a torch. But why? He glanced out to sea, searching for a responding light or even a confirming sound. There was nothing. He knew here against the house side they could easily be seen by anyone emerging from the gorse, so he couldn't wait.

Quietly, and with a practised ease, Kirkgordon

swung round to the front of the house. The front steps, which had seemed well built from the previous elevation, were broken and provided no foothold. With a delicate jump followed by a silent landing, he moved to the balcony. Gliding up to the window he tried to peer in but the glass was filthy and covered in the most part by a curtain of a greenish hue. The whole building felt like it was about to crumble, felt uninhabited. But the aerial?

Scuttling under the window, Kirkgordon moved to the front door. It was slightly ajar. Paint peeled off its sides and the ripening wind was making it swing, but no sound was coming from its rusty looking hinges. Someone needs the silence. But why? To stop someone looking, or to hear an intruder's step? This was not normal. The victim walks in. No sound from the door which would halt their track. They would walk right into a trap.

Kirkgordon racked his memory of the side of the house. Were there any holes? Look-outs? Did they know he was coming? He had no option. They needed to take the chance of finding a radio. Well, he wasn't going to present an easy target.

Stepping to the door's edge, he knelt down. Beckoned forward, Calandra crept to the other side of the door. Kirkgordon waited for a particularly strong gust of wind. As the door swung open slightly, he used the edge of his bow to continue its progress until it was fully open. As luck would have it, the door remained open. He drew the bow back, primed it and glanced inside. There was nothing this side of the door. His eyes quickly read shadows as cups and pots, chairs and clocks. Kirkgordon shook his head at Calandra. Now he rotated onto his back, drawing his feet up before planting them on the ground. With a deft but firm push he slid backwards into the room.

Top left, fish eyes. Two arrows buried deep. Far right, a figure, small but with trident. Primed and drawn. Fingers released. Child! With lightning reactions he pulled the bow left and the arrow shot past the child's ear.

"Mr Kirkgordon, enough. We are secure. Call Calandra in." The tension snapped like a broken drawstring. "We don't have long. And no, there's no radio. Not a working one, anyway."

Chapter 21

Plans

"Dammit, Havers, I could have killed the child!"

"And I am glad to say that you did not, Mr Kirkgordon. Let me introduce you to young James, son of a Mr Macleod who is currently offshore, availing himself of the work offered on the north sea oil rigs. His mother is here, Mrs Donaldina Macleod. She's upstairs, trying to tend to Mr Austerley's wounds."

"Austerley's alive!"

"How is he?" said Calandra, brushing in past Kirkgordon.

"Somewhat bruised and battered, as the expression goes, but physically... operational. Mentally... somewhat compromised."

"What the hell happened? You were meant to be lying low." Calandra hurried upstairs while young James just stood and stared at Kirkgordon. It was somewhat off-putting, but Kirkgordon didn't feel he had the right to complain after nearly piercing the child's head.

James was a stout young man, possibly twelve years of age. Dressed in black jeans with a T-shirt brandishing the logo of a heavy metal band, his hair was close-cropped. His face was sombre and worried, but with his father away he was fronting up as the alpha male in the family.

"We ran into a spot of bother; hence the fish-head you saw fit to bury your arrows into. James, my good man, be so good as to get a cup of tea for Mr Kirkgordon and one for Miss Calandra. In fact, check if your mother and Mr Austerley require one. Good chap."

James turned away with no acknowledgement and was soon climbing the small flight of stairs.

"So what happened? Cally said you could look after yourself."

"Your friend and I are here, alive, and with all appendages accounted for. The mental injury is quite removed from my actions. I dare say you may have struggled to achieve the same result." Havers' eyes narrowed in a questioning look.

"Havers, I'm not criticizing! We ran into a frog-man out there. Took both of us to take him out. In fact, he roughed Cally up a bit. Her leg's seized up even more. She's struggling to walk."

"I am aware of that. I saw you carry her here.

You forgot to scan for eyeholes in the wall. It's a good job I was watching your back. The torch drew you inside, as I hoped. My apologies for a lack of warning, but I believe some of the creatures have remarkable hearing. You did well to get here."

"I saw the radio. Does it work?"

Havers shook his head before turning as James entered with a mug of tea, which he handed to Kirkgordon.

"Thanks, son. Sorry for the arrow. It's been a bit of a rough ride so far."

"Can you get my mum out of here?" James stared at Kirkgordon, who felt his usefulness was being questioned.

"Honestly, I don't know. But I'll try."

"Sit down, James, my lad. You may have some useful information for us. And you should know all that is going on. Mr Kirkgordon is about to tell me of his tour of the village. He may have some answers."

Gripping the hot tea like a school prize, Kirkgordon told of their exploits that evening, from the pictures and the manuscript to the missing items from the table, the crowd outside Elliot's and the encounter with the frog-man. Havers sat motionless, listening, but James widened his eyes in horror at the story. Once the tale was complete, Havers stood and walked to the window. They remained in darkness, but he wasn't looking for anything; instead, he was deep in thought.

Kirkgordon turned to James, who was now trembling a little. "It's okay, son, feeling afraid is okay. We're all scared. Even Havers is shit scared."

"Language, Mr Kirkgordon. Let's set the youth of today a more expressive example than that American vulgarity."

Kirkgordon rolled his eyes and James let out a little laugh. Years of working in the field had taught Kirkgordon of the need to let out the pent-up fear when you could. Kids being caught up in bad situations was nothing new to him, but the current issues were not exactly typical.

"How long have you been here, James?"

"Six months. Dad had saved up from being offshore to get us an island house for Mum. She's got nerves, you see. Really bad ones, so the doctor says."

Oh magic, thought Kirkgordon.

"So we came somewhere quiet," James continued. "And it is quiet here. But the school was weird. There was no RE. Not that I minded. Lots of history about America, places in New England. Always on about fishing and reefs."

"That is strange. What did your folks say about it?"

"They complained, but the headmaster just said that was the way it was. It was all in the curriculum. They took it to the mainland as well, but they haven't got back yet. I tried not to make a big deal of it cos of Mum. She was struggling as it was." James hung his head in silence.

"Why? What happened to her?"

"This place. That's what happened. We're not one of them, see. They have all these weird festivals going on, dressing up like fish and things. Marching up and down the village. I'm just glad we're all the way out here. I went once to see one of the festivals but they chased me away. I saw a man dressed in a robe with a frog's head. It was just weird. Teacher asked what I had seen. Said it was just a made-up man and to forget it." James went quiet. However, Kirkgordon could see he was fighting the urge to ask a question.

"Careful, James. Make sure you want the answer before you ask."

James started to tremble. "You said you killed a frog-man. You didn't mean a diver, did you?"

Kirkgordon stepped over to James and put his arms around him. Then, taking James' face in his hands, he looked deep into the child's eyes. He shook his head and whispered, "No." The floodgates broke and James started to weep. His body racked and convulsed with horror and all Kirkgordon could do was hold him. For a moment, he was taken back to his own children, when he had had to explain he was going away for a while, after the incident. None of the horrors of the grave or even his previous profession had prepared him for the sheer abjectness of his kids' suffering.

"James, why don't you go and see to your mum? Make sure she's okay. Mr Austerley can be quite draining on people. Good lad!" prompted Havers.

When the boy could be heard climbing the stairs, Havers came over and sat down in front of Kirkgordon. Normally Havers was a picture of calm, the eye of the storm, but now this bastion of serenity looked worried.

"They have trashed the radio. There's a hidey-hole under the stairs which leads to a tunnel to no-one-knows-where. The boy and his mother hid in there when they came. From what they said, it was almost directly after they came in on Mr Austerley and myself at the pub. The poor lad had to hold onto his mother, almost smothering her in the effort to keep her quiet."

"What's the plan? Tell me you have a plan, cos I'm all out, Havers."

"I have been trying to signal my boatman to come ashore, but he seems to be singularly failing in responding."

"He's dead. Found him on the shore about a mile or two back. Not pretty. Most of his face was gone."

"It would appear that we are the sum hope for sorting out this little mess, then. The satellite phone won't connect, some kind of interference. Did you go by the harbour? Were there any vessels we could procure?"

"Nothing, and anyway, that's where the frog-man was. If we go out into the sea, Havers, we're goners! These things are pretty good on land, but in the water, they'd be devastating. Austerley said something about some cataclysmic event. Any ideas where and when?"

"Where is here. This island. When was going to be about now until their plans hit a snag. We were very fortunate."

"Why? What happened?"

Havers looked thoughtful for a moment before

beginning his tale in soft tones. "After Miss Calandra and yourself left on your scouting trip, Mr Austerley continued to babble somewhat. Then he became violently agitated, kicking out and screaming, Mother Hydra, Mother Hydra. Then one word, over and over again: Dagon. There was an inhuman strength in him and, despite my expertise in restraining techniques, he threw me into the wall. Admittedly, the distance was not excessive but the strength with which he completed the action was remarkable. How much do you know about the Eldars?" Havers pursed his lips and looked hard into Kirkgordon's eyes.

"Well, I did meet them. Ask Austerley!"

"No, Mr Kirkgordon, you did not meet them. What you met were mere minions of these things."

Kirkgordon stared in disbelief. "Minions?"

"Yes, minions. The masters and lords of those creatures are quite something else. They are usually held back from a full appearance here on earth, but at certain times they can be released. We are in one of those times. That's why Mr Austerley is somewhat agitated."

"Austerley? Are you saying he's connected to this?"

"Mr Austerley is somewhat sensitive to the Eldars. At times like these, times when an Elder could be summoned forth to our existence, people of a certain disposition become attached... no, attuned to certain beings. They become entwined with their thoughts and sometimes actions. If they pursue these beings and expose themselves to these impulses, then certain knowledge can be passed to them. It is rarely of a nature beneficial to themselves or our human race."

"So Austerley's a problem?"

"A problem and, possibly, a solution. Bear with me and I will explain. Austerley's agitations caused the folk in the pub to come to our room. Clearly, they recognized his connection, his previous showing downstairs contributing, no doubt, to their suspicions. I was indisposed with Mr Austerley, trying to contain his ramblings, when I heard a knock on the door. Being occupied, I told them to try again later when I would be able to attend to their inquiry. However, the door was rudely opened and in strode the robed gentleman who had been rather abrupt with ourselves in the bar.

"On seeing the man again, Austerley started to yell and weep on the floor, screaming out E-O-D, E-O-D. Behind the robed man, a few of the locals tried to barge into the room but only caused confusion due to the limited dimensions. The robed man tripped and fell onto Austerley, who kicked and lashed out in a rather effective manner, causing the individual to yell for assistance. Austerley, meantime, had ripped off the emblem on the robe and declared doom to all because of the Order represented."

"Ah yes, the Entwined Order of Divinity!"

"Hardly, Mr Kirkgordon. The Esoteric Order of Dagon! A name I only remember because Mr Austerley brought its very roots back to me with his constantly agitated rambling as he kicked out. First

Elliot's, La Fayette, Washington Avenue; but then he continued: Gilman house hotel, Allen said it, Zadok said it. Mr Kirkgordon, we are talking about Innsmouth!"

Kirkgordon looked bemused. "Innsmouth. What the hell is Innsmouth?"

"Where, Mr Kirkgordon, where. An old seaport in New England and a serious place of trouble for our American cousins some hundred years ago. There was a cull there, by our friends in the FBI, of some very dangerous customs and creatures. People that became fish-like and frog-like through their worship of Dagon. It appears that some of the Innsmouth folk got out – and they seem to have migrated here. You saw some of them on the pictures in the church. And you encountered one, hand to hand. If my suspicions, or rather Mr Austerley's suspicions, are correct, this place is overrun with them."

"You said Austerley was both a solution and a problem. How come?"

"Well, unfortunately, the man in the robe got quite aggressive towards Mr Austerley and regrettably I had to remove him from the room." Havers lifted his eyebrows.

"The broken window. So the blood on the ground belonged to the man in the robe, not you or Austerley."

"Some of the blood on the ground was Mr Austerley's."

"The robed guy got to him then? Gave him a crack?"

"No, I did. I had to shut him up and find an exit from the situation. In his hysterical state, Mr Austerley was compromising that objective." Havers showed no sign of emotion, just pure practicality. "Other men then tried to occupy the room but I managed to force them away. Unfortunately, my gun was taken in the process."

"But didn't they trail you?"

"Once on the ground I spotted Mr Austerley's bleeding mouth and placed my handkerchief into it. The handkerchief appeared to perform both functions required of it more than adequately."

"But why is he a problem?"

"When we were on the ground, turning to proceed clear of the building, a face appeared at the window. Mr Austerley recognized him immediately. His visage was similar to mine but this time he was not wearing a suit. I believe you have had trouble with him before."

"Farthington! He's here?" Kirkgordon was wide-eyed with horror.

"It would appear so. Hence, Mr Austerley is compromised." Havers drew a grim face.

"I'm not with you, Havers."

"Mr Austerley, when he screamed about the Esoteric Order of Dagon, was even more concerned when he saw the man in the robe. He recognized the colours as belonging to One Who Is The Gateway. The events that are to happen need a person like this."

"Then we're in luck, as he's dead."

"Yes... and no. There is someone who has the

link, someone who has read that book, someone who understands all the ins and outs, all the ceremonies, the precursors, the elements necessary. Someone who can take the man's place."

"Austerley."

"Exactly, Mr Kirkgordon. And Mr Farthington knows this. When they interrogated him they learnt a lot. Not the secrets to unlock, but rather the potency of, the mind of Mr Austerley. Turned the wrong way, Mr Austerley is lethal to the cause of everything good and decent. I have considered just dispatching him."

"No!" Kirkgordon scoured Havers' face looking for any pretence of drama, or a humorous context being drawn upon, but none was forthcoming. Havers was his usual calm, dispassionate self. "So why not, Havers? What's stopping you?"

"Because it would not stop them, only slow them down. There are others. There will be other moments to release these beings. And I would probably condemn everyone, including myself, to an early grave. The problem would continue. When I finish things, Mr Kirkgordon, I finish them completely."

"So what's your plan?"

"From my conversations with Mr Austerley, I know there is a time during the summoning ceremony that the portal being used to bring forth the creature can be closed forever. Mr Austerley knows how. But we need to get him close."

"You're going to give him up. Let them place him in the ceremony."

"Yes. They will come here for Mr Austerley. They will take him. The rest of us are in danger, for we are of no use to them."

"What about the tunnel James and his mum hid in? Is there a way out through there?"

"No, it's blocked. I've been holding here, trying to get Mr Austerley on board with the plan. I've also been trying to heal him. Miss Calandra will help with that. She's very good with wounds. An impressive old woman!"

"So we need to move out. That's a risk. Havers, are you sure about Austerley? He's liable to conjure this thing up just to get a photo of it for his scrapbook. Trust me, he's not stable!"

"That's why we need to be there. Why you need to be there. You'll need to do the necessary if he can't hold it together. I know he's your friend. But I know you will do it. You can be as dispassionate as me when you need to."

"No, I can't," said Kirkgordon, turning away from Havers, "but I will do what needs to be done. And he's not my friend, he's just the poor bastard who screwed up my marriage." Kirkgordon stared into the blackness of the room. "And what if this thing gets loose, what then?"

"Then, Mr Kirkgordon, you pray, and seek a higher power to deal with it. There is no blackness like this being. One of the Eldars and supremely powerful, mighty Dagon will wreak a darkness over this earth."

Suddenly Kirkgordon burst out laughing.

"I don't think you are taking me seriously, Mr

Kirkgordon."

"Dagon is one-nil down against my God, Mr Havers. And my God uses the weak. Austerley's going to be perfect, just perfect!"

Chapter 22

Donaldina

Austerley had calmed down from his ramblings but it took a good two hours before he was fully coherent. Kirkgordon had wondered how Havers had extracted so much information from him but surmised Havers was well versed in the background of all this madness.

Certainly, Havers seemed to be accurate on most counts, and regarding Calandra he was certainly correct. A remarkable job had been done on Austerley to make him seem almost human again after his wounds from the encounter with the robed man. Indeed, when Havers explained his plan to Austerley, he seemed positively excited.

"The one thing we don't know is the site for the

summoning," explained Havers, "so we'll have to keep good tabs on you, Mr Austerley. Between your friends and I, I dare say that shouldn't be a problem. Once we have closed the portal, we'll need to be about ourselves and find an exit off this rock. The Innsmouth settlers will not be on friendly terms with us and we'll need a small army to keep them quiet. So if anyone should see a boat or an escape of any sort then speak up."

"Excuse me, Mr Havers?"

"Yes, James, my boy?"

"Well, I don't know of any boats, but there's an aeroplane on the far side of the island. Mr Mackenzie had it before he walked off the rocks that night. He used to go up in it a lot, but it's been in his shed since then. At least, the frame is; he used to keep the wing separate as he told me that it was really expensive, and he didn't want the frogs getting it."

"Whereabouts is this place, James?" asked Havers calmly.

"On round from here... maybe, what, two mile, Mum?"

Mrs Macleod nodded. "But it's not safe, Mr Havers! That's where old Mackenzie said he saw them walking fish. I used to think he was drunk. He was such a laugh down the social... but with the drink and that... well, no one believed him."

"It's okay, Mrs Macleod," said Calandra, putting her arms around the woman, who had buried her face in her hands, weeping intensely.

"Gotta be an option, Havers?" said Kirkgordon.

"I know a lot about aircraft," Austerley beamed. "I could probably get that thing going!"

"No, Mr Austerley, your path is set. Perhaps I could turn a hand with young James. I'm an ex-RAF engineer, you know!" It was Havers' turn to show a bit of pride.

"Then you should go, Havers," Kirkgordon said. "It's an option that needs to be pursued. We'll take care of Mrs Macleod and then get after Austerley. After all, I'm always his wingman!"

Austerley grimaced at Kirkgordon before looking over at Calandra and smiling. "It's fine. I have Calandra watching me." Calandra played the enchanted party but deep down she knew she was merely protection for Kirkgordon. It would be his arrows that would take down Austerley in the case of failure.

"Agreed," said Havers. "James, say goodbye to your mother and get a warm, dark coat. Don't worry, madam, I'll take care of him."

Mother and child embraced deeply while Kirkgordon worked out how they should leave Austerley in the house. They didn't want to make their plan obvious. Calandra took a secretive peek out of the front door.

"Churchy, the footprints are covered up. It's still snowing quite heavily."

"Good. Havers," called Kirkgordon, before the government man could exit the house, "take the boy on your shoulders for the first mile. It'll look like you've left Austerley behind. It'll keep the boy out of their hunt too."

"An excellent idea, Mr Kirkgordon." Havers took Kirkgordon's arm and drew him aside. "You know I can't wait for any of you. Once it's working, I have to go. There are no guarantees for the boy, either."

"I know. Just hide him well. I'll come get him. And I'll try to indicate where the gate is for the cavalry when they come."

"Do that, Mr Kirkgordon, otherwise they'll have to wipe out everything. And I mean everything."

"Understood. And Havers..." Kirkgordon extended a hand. "God guide you."

"And the best of British luck to you, sir."

Within thirty seconds, James was riding on Havers' back out of the house and across the deepening snow. Mrs Macleod watched her son until Calandra pulled her back into the house, scanning the horizon for signs of anything fishy.

"Okay, Indy, time to get your make-up on," said Kirkgordon. "Lie down on the floor. Mrs Macleod, get a flask and head down into the tunnel. Calandra and I will join you shortly."

"Felt safer with Havers around," grumbled Austerley. "Didn't get bloody singed with him."

You stupid arse, thought Kirkgordon. Havers would put a bullet in your head if necessary. All this over a woman I'm trying to keep away from.

"Come on," said Calandra, "lie down and I'll sort you out." Like a lamb, Austerley obeyed, and soon Calandra was opening up some of his facial wounds, letting small amounts of blood trickle across his face. She calmed his pained look with several delicate kisses to his temple. Kirkgordon threw some furniture about and placed some props beneath Austerley's head.

"It'll look like Havers has gone for help. Just don't get up."

"All right! Just let me be."

"And remember. Close the gateway! That's all that matters."

"What the hell do you think I am? Some sort of clown? I know what to do. In fact, I'm the only one who knows. For all your weapons and talk, who knows how to deal with all this? Me, flippin' me. So get off your high horse, you perfectly heroic arse-head!"

"I'll deal with this. Get to the tunnel," Calandra whispered to Kirkgordon. She knelt beside Austerley and gently caressed his head, rubbing the back of his neck. Kirkgordon turned and strode away, praying to God he wouldn't need to use an arrow. He swore he could hear Calandra singing.

Mrs Macleod was sitting quietly, if anxiously, in the small tunnel beneath the stairs. A flask of tea sat beside her with three mugs, a nip of milk and some digestive biscuits. She smiled at Kirkgordon as he clambered in beside her, placing his quiver and bow within easy reach.

"Thank you."

"For what?"

"Being here. Helping us. It's like the worst nightmare you can imagine. Living amongst them has been so crushing. Soul-destroying. They look at you like you're the spawn of hell. Total ignorance and loathing. Funny though, turns out it's them that's the spawn of hell. Frasier said he didn't like them. He never trusted them. Funny eyes, he said. And they have. Never realized how funny." Mrs Macleod breathed in deeply, settling her nerves back down again.

"Frasier?" asked Kirkgordon.

"My man. James' father. He won't have a clue. Telephone's not working, either. He'll think it's a power cut or something. Still, he's better clear of it. James is better away too. Maybe he'll get away with that Mr Havers. Very polite man. Good man, I think."

Kirkgordon knew not to destroy hope at these times. "I'm sure you're a good judge of character." As long as there's room for two on the plane. Poor kid. Still, he'd be a sitting duck if we hadn't found them.

"Are you married, Mr Kirkgordon?" asked Mrs Macleod, interrupting his train of thought.

"Yes, yes, I am. To Alana." Alana's face rolled into view.

"That's nice. Children?"

"Two. Peter and Ruth. Both under ten." Again, he could see them clearly.

"Are you close, you and Alana?"

"It's been difficult. My work, it... gets in the way."

Mrs Macleod nodded sagely. "Time away always does. Frasier was difficult when he started the rigs. Never felt home was his own. Was it time away that hurt your relationship?"

"No, not really. I just... I just... well, let's say... I brought my work home with me."

They sat side by side in silence, each lost in deep thoughts of their better halves. Kirkgordon saw the curve of Alana's shoulders, the long T-shirt she would wear when she really wanted him. He saw the wonder in her eyes when they "rocked the Kasbah", as she put it. How he wanted to be back there right now. How he needed to be there. To hold her as they watched their young ones sleeping. He would not let this darkness take them away.

"Do you pray, Mr Kirkgordon?"

"Well, they do call me Churchy," laughed Kirkgordon, "but it's been a while. We ain't been on great terms."

"He's always with me, Mr Kirkgordon. Never left me through all this. Even when Frasier had the trouble with that woman. He'll see me through, and you too. He's on your side, Churchy!"

"I pray you're right... what's your first name?"

"Donaldina."

"Thank you, Donaldina."

She took his hand in hers and quietly spoke to her God for the next five minutes in a whispered voice. Protection for them all and a vanquishing of this darkness were her major themes. Often, she would clench tightly Kirkgordon's hand. When he opened his eyes, Calandra was crouching before them, head bowed.

"Cup of tea, dear?"

"Thank you. Just black please, Mrs Macleod."

"Donaldina, dear. Just Donaldina."

"Cally. Just Cally."

"Is Austerley set?" asked Kirkgordon.

"Yes. He's good. Don't worry, he knows what we're into. Have some faith, Churchy."

The tunnel was tight and Calandra had to sit down on Kirkgordon's knees, sending that chilled ripple through his body. It was time to wait for the search party to find them. Slowly his eyes adjusted to the darkness of the tunnel, and behind him Kirkgordon was able to see the rockfall which blocked the way. Not an easy job, but he reckoned the obstruction was removable, although some extra time would be required.

Time seemed to expand in the darkness, and Kirkgordon was glad of his watch to keep track of it. His mind drifted back to Alana and those precious moments of intimacy. And yet, sat on him was a woman who was in so many ways so similar. Cally especially reminded him of the Alana he had first met; she had her shoulders too. He longed to have that Alana back, but he knew time and circumstance may have sent her away forever.

Then they heard it. The front door burst open. From the sound of it, the hinges were in extreme danger of losing their mountings. Then footsteps, and something else. It took Kirkgordon a moment before he connected the sound with a hop, hop, hop motion. Then voices. Agitated, quite loud too. But in a foreign language. No, not foreign. Alien, unknown. Like the smacking of pouting lips. Like a... Kirkgordon felt sick... a fish. And then another voice. Damn it, if that wasn't a croak of some sort.

Then a human voice. Well, a dry, rasping, near-croak of a voice. It was telling Austerley to get up. Then the heavy footsteps. Austerley's elephantine plodding. And a hop, hop, hop. And the slam of the door.

Calandra turned her head to look at Kirkgordon. He shook his head. She waited. The wind was evidently whirling outside. Kirkgordon imagined more snow falling, covering up the departing party of evil. Calandra looked at him again. Another shake of the head. He could feel her tensing. Still just the wind. Everything else was ever so quiet. She looked again. And he nodded.

Calandra delicately and quietly tiptoed to the entrance under the stairs and cautiously opened the door. Nothing was seen or heard and Kirkgordon watched her close the door behind her, staff in hand.

There was no sound of footsteps, but Kirkgordon knew Calandra would go upstairs, seeking the best viewing hole to trace where Austerley and his captors had gone. He watched his timepiece tick by. She would be coming down soon. Yes, about now. A quick walk to the front room to check all was clear. Then turn round and... thud! The dullest of thuds. Then a light body hitting the ground and the clattering of a wooden staff onto the floor. And a croak that seemed full of delight.

Chapter 23

Saved by Innocence

Havers was running hard. His breath condensed in the cold air as he fought his way through the now fully developed blizzard. James was holding on tight, occasionally pointing out directions. It had been a while since such a consistent run had been demanded of him, but Havers was up to the task. He prided himself on his neat physique and methodical yet innovative approach to his work. But now he was facing one of his sternest tests, and it would be of a mechanical nature.

The young lad was good, thought Havers. Not a single complaint even though he was frightened. It was hard to imagine growing up in a place like this. Feeling like an outcast was bad enough, but for rumours and tales of fish-men and frog-men to be commonplace, and for Mr Mackenzie to die in those strange circumstances... it was a wonder the kid's nerves were holding.

Havers' pace did not decline even when hitting slopes and valleys through several of the dunes. The sand was mixed in with the fallen snow and his grip was unsure. Several times he stumbled but compensated with small half-steps to keep his rhythm going. James clung on tight, making him an easier burden to carry than most. Panting hard, Havers rounded the bottom of a dune before desperately diving to his left, into the sand. James went to cry out, but a firm hand covered his mouth.

Up ahead was a quaint, grey pebble-dashed two-storey house with the typical sloping roof of the islands. One side was a perfect white from the snow, and visible against that festive backdrop was a pair of spindly legs, a broad torso and a bloated head with enormous eyes. Blast, thought Havers, I was hoping to get to the place clean.

"James, I am going to ask a few questions," said Havers, deep into the child's ear, "and all I require of you is a shake or nod of the head. Do you understand?"

James nodded.

"Good. That house ahead, is that the one we are looking for?"

Again a nod.

"Is the plane in the house?"

A shake.

"Is it nearer the sea?"

Negative.

"Further inland?"

Negative.

"Then where?"

A arm extended and, with a cupping motion, James indicated the rear of the house.

"In a barn?"

A nod.

"Good. As you can see there is a frog-man at the house. I doubt he is alone but I need to scout to make sure. If you are with me, it will not work. So I need you to hide out here. Can you do that?"

A pained face stared back at Havers and he could see the child's terror. But a grim nod was returned. Havers took James' hand and led him round the back of the dune telling him to lie down and to watch the house. He would return for him when it was safe. Havers wished he could advise what to do if he didn't come back, but he didn't know.

It took Havers a good twenty minutes to successfully skirt the perimeter of the house. There were three would-be guards on duty: two frog-men and one human. Kirkgordon would be useful now, thought Havers, using his arrows to dispatch these threats. He would have to do it the hard way.

So far he had kept his distance, knowing his current garb would be easily seen up close. Deep down, Havers felt the thrill of adventure again. Too long he had been behind the desk, pulling the strings, giving the orders; now he felt like the agent who had wet his ears deep behind the Russian border during that cold war. He felt it was fitting that, now so enlivened, he was once again working alongside Calandra. He had aged but he had also matured, and what had been taken by his departing youth was made up for with that seasoning. He took the garrotte from his jacket and prepared to approach.

Coming in from the side of the house in shadow, Havers quietly walked up to the back of the first frog-man. He watched carefully, keeping himself directly in line with the back of its head, worried in case those eyes had a field of vision much greater than his own. On silent feet, he crept the last few steps before throwing the garrotte around the frog-man's large throat, catching it in his free hand and pulling hard, satisfied when he heard a distinctive click. Havers held the garrotte tight while the frog-man struggled for breath before becoming limp and decidedly heavy to hold. The lifeless lump was allowed to fall.

Breathe in and out. Calm, thought Havers, always calm. The government employee glided to the edge of the building, aware that on turning the corner he would be in whatever light was coming through the storm. Flicking his head ever so briefly round the corner, he glimpsed the remaining two guards. Havers pulled a small knife from within his garments and prepared to assail his foes. With the frog-man's strength, he knew he would have to be quick.

Rounding the corner in full sprint, Havers threw the knife straight into the throat of the human guard. Before the body had toppled to the ground, he was leaping into the frog-man, lashing out at its chest with a kick. The beast fell to the ground and Havers followed up by throwing the garrotte around its throat, but the creature had instinctively thrown an arm in front of its face and the garrotte wrapped around this arm instead. The beast slammed its arm into the ground and Havers was thrown down in front of the creature, his shoulder driving hard into the snow followed by his head banging on to the cold, hard surface.

Trying to roll back up, Havers barely managed to get to his knees. His breathing was racing now, pulling frosty air into his lungs. Beyond the need for air, his impulses were a groggy fog of confusion. Then he felt the slimy, long-fingered arms around his throat. Instinctively, his hands shot to the arms of the creature, trying to drive them off. Slowly, he felt a slight release in the pressure before a slap to the back of the head drove his face into the ground. Again his throat was grabbed and this time, with his opponent behind him, all he could do was reach for the fingers themselves. His grip slipped off the creature's hands time and again. His body started to panic despite his efforts at controlled breathing, and he lashed out with his arms to little effect. Flat on the ground with his opponent over him, Havers felt the cold, sinking reality of a life finishing.

There was a squelching sound, rather like plunging your hands into jelly. And then a sound of an uncontrolled croak, mixed with a rasping howl. Then a wetness soaking the back of his neck. The pressure released from his throat but instead he was crushed under a falling frog-man. Pushing back hard and kicking intensely, Havers freed himself from the body which was pressing down on him and rolled to his feet, staggering from lack of oxygen.

James was lying in the snow a few feet away, his hands covered in blackish blood, most of which had emerged from the prone frog-man's body. Havers' small knife was buried in the frog-man's head. With a few deep breaths came the return of his trained reactions. Havers surveyed the area to see the dead human guard lying on the ground, the knife no longer in his throat.

The child was frozen statue-like in shock so Havers picked him up and took him inside the house. Returning outside, he retrieved all three bodies and dumped them into the dark recesses of the house. In the front room, James was sat on the floor staring blankly ahead. Havers approached quietly and sat down beside him. The smell of the viscous blood on the back of his neck was attacking his nostrils, but he withheld his disgust, preferring to try to comfort the boy. Never having had children, the action felt awkward, but the long-time agent wrapped his arms around James who broke into a fit of crying, sporadically exploding with exaggerated coughs like a clapped-out car.

Time almost seemed irrelevant while they were embracing, Havers only wanting to bring the boy back to a semblance of normality. Slowly, and with the occasional recurrence, James became a more composed, if somewhat paler, child.

"We need to keep going, James. We need this

aeroplane to resolve this situation. We can get rid of this evil but I need you to be strong. Can you do that?"

A nod.

"Good boy. And, James? Thank you. You saved my life. Do you understand that? You saved me. It was me or that thing and you saved me. I won't lie to you, you will think about this a lot. But you did the right thing. Thank you."

James managed a faint smile.

"Good. Now, shall we go out to the building where the aeroplane is?"

James stood up and went to open the door but Havers gently held him back. Opening the door first by the slightest margin, and then with increasing confidence, Havers guided James out into the night before letting him show the path to the barn on the far side of the house. His head hurt from being tossed into the ground, but Havers focused hard and entered the barn only after sweeping the perimeter and deftly clearing the inside. Once he was happy no one was there, he led James in and prompted him.

"Where's the aeroplane, James?"

The barn itself was only large enough to hold about two cars and had a corrugated iron roof with brick walls. There was no obvious source of heating and the barn wall accommodated a mass of old dust-covered tools. Various empty boxes littered the floor and a brown, tatty boiler suit hung from a rusted nail. A green tarpaulin covered a unknown object against the far wall.

James ran over to the tarpaulin and, with a heave, pulled it back from the item beneath. There was a long green wing of light material supported by a skeleton frame of aluminium. A small cockpit with three wheels had a large propeller sitting against it.

"Is this the aeroplane, James?"

A nod.

Blast it, thought Havers, it's a microlight. With the winds outside it'll be a difficult flight. There's no way to take more than two, and more likely one, person. I'd better check for fuel.

There were a couple of jerrycans at the far end of the room amongst some paints. Havers lifted them and was delighted to find that one was full and the other about half-full. His head thumped, his shoulder ached and he had a petrified child for assistance. But memories of play and an old sixties television show came to mind. Havers' inner child spoke: "I wanna be Scotty! I'll see what I can do, Captain!"

Chapter 24

Dangling Choices

Calandra was compromised. That much was clear. Kirkgordon crept forward to the tunnel door and listened intently. Mrs Macleod had her hand over her mouth, her body visibly shaking from all manner of ghastly thoughts racing through her head. Keeping his clear of such distractions, Kirkgordon picked out at least four different creatures. Various hoppings and shufflings led him to the conclusion that there was a mix of creatures but probably not any humans.

Loath to open the door in case he betrayed their location, Kirkgordon was left helpless to intervene. He heard no "killing blow" but instead much conversation in croaks and babbles. All the time,

Austerley was being led further away. Indecision drilled at his mind. Was it more important to help Calandra or track Austerley? He knew what Havers' choice would be. But Havers hadn't been rescued by this woman, sporting her black wings in devastating fashion; hadn't been whisked away by her from the claws of a fire-breathing dragon; hadn't been propositioned by her, mesmerized by her pale beauty; hadn't bonded with her as another of life's cast-offs.

So he waited. Judging by the vocal exchanges and the bumps and scrapings on the floor, Cally had been picked up and dragged off. Then he heard a scream, just barely, before it was muffled. Then came a slight commotion, some hopping and shuffling with occasional tandem sounds and then the sound of the door opening. The seashell to your ear; that was it, thought Kirkgordon. That was the sound of the wind tonight. The snowstorm still raged and they had gone out into it. And left the door open.

Now he was in a quandary. Had they left another guard? Dare he wait? The snow had been falling rapidly beforehand, so the likelihood of losing track of Calandra, and certainly Austerley, increased with every second's delay. And what about Mrs Macleod? This was risking her life too. Finally his fondness for Calandra overpowered all thoughts of remaining hidden and he gently opened the tunnel door.

Nothing could be seen in the dark of the hallway where the tunnel entrance opened out beneath the stairs. Silently, Kirkgordon glided to the door of the front room, scanning all around for any untoward shadows. He drew his bow. The only sounds were the wildness of the wind and the thump of his beating heart. Turning the corner, he checked the front room, which was empty. Retreating, he took in the kitchen, then the stairs, before completing a quick reconnaissance of the upper floor. Only then did he deem it safe to return to the tunnel and speak to Mrs Macleod.

"Stay here, Donaldina. Whatever happens, do not open this door, and stay as far back in the tunnel as possible. I'll come back for you when it's safe. And pray! Whatever you have in you, please, just pray!" Donaldina nodded knowingly and settled herself down for a long wait. Now that would be hell for me, thought Kirkgordon, just hoping and relying on others.

With practised ease, Kirkgordon exited the building, surveying his surroundings at all times. There was only one group of footprints, or rather flipper-prints, leaving the house, and he raced along their trail. Soon he was amongst the dunes he had traced his way through with Calandra, and it was here that the single group of prints became two. Only one set contained human prints; that must be Austerley. The prints were also somewhat fainter. Kirkgordon took a nearby stick and laid it on the ground pointing in the direction of the markings. Satisfied with his signal, he hurried off in search of Calandra's captors. As he ran, Kirkgordon's lungs drew in and pumped out air at a rate sustained only by repetitive practice. Although worried about losing Austerley's trail, it occurred to him that while these amphibian foes could leap and hop about over a short range in a fashion equal to, if not better than, a human, they were unlikely to sustain a man's pace over longer, uneven terrain. He felt a deep chill across his face, battered by the wind and the driving snow. He realized that he was retracing his route back toward the village. Despite having been in this direction only once, Kirkgordon's sense of place was ringing loud that the harbour was up ahead; he knew the next corner would be his exit from the dunes onto the exposed harbour front. Kirkgordon dived into the grassy verge and crawled through the snow to the dune-top to check if his progress was clear. The scene presented was not an encouraging one.

Calandra was starting to feel the blood rushing to her head. Her long hair was hanging limply beneath her and her hands were tied incredibly tightly behind her back at waist height. The thick rope was cutting into her wrists and she was sure blood was running down her arms inside her jacket. Looking up, she saw her feet bound to a metal pole with more coarse rope. She heard the waves crashing into the wall below, and a fine mist of spray made her hair damp.

A scarf was tied round her mouth, preventing her from shouting out. Her ears could hear the excited croaks and babbling of what she believed to be her abductors. The harbour wall was behind her and she was looking out to sea. The previous mist had now been replaced by driving snow which melted on contact with the water; still the visibility was a only a kilometre. At that distance, the waves were black, rotating surfaces, like constantly changing Rubik's cubes which had had their colourful stickers removed.

In her younger days she had lived near the coast and had, on many a day, stood and watched with great comfort the passing of the tide. Throughout her life, it had helped heal moments of despair and frustration with its reassuringly slow, rhythmic beat. But all she felt now was an overwhelming sense of failure.

Calandra cried, not in fear of her life but for the lack of friendship and closeness in her final moments. Austerley, who had once amused and treasured her; Havers, who had seen past her freakish coldness; and dear Churchy. He had thought so much of her, not taking from her what he could not return. Now, with no pillar to hold on to, she mourned the ending of a cursed life which had driven so many loves away.

Then in the distance, she saw it. Revealed only when the tide dipped was a rounded, buoy-like figure, six foot of it showing with every swell. It would have been a mere curiosity but for the pair of eyes that was focused on the harbour, unblinking through every wave. Calandra's heart froze at the sight of a long tentacle bursting out of the ocean, revealing the suckered underside. It had all the

Crescendo!

markings of an octopus, but never had she seen such a look of human intent in a creature's eyes.

Fighting for something to think about apart from the horror of being bait for this creature, Calandra calculated she had approximately two minutes before the sea-beast reached her hanging point. She started to swing on her bindings but they were too secure, every frantic motion causing the rope to bite harder into her ankles. Unable to see her captors, she could hear what she suspected was laughter. A cacophony of croaks and bubbling noises in which there was an unmistakeable vehemence.

But then it stopped. The creature was still approaching, yet there was silence behind her. It was as if someone had struck the mute button on the frog-men by accident. Except there was one sound, just discernible above the waves. Like a hopping. But different to that she had heard before.

Despite the approaching horror, Calandra's curiosity drove her to twist hard and try to catch a glimpse of what was fascinating her abductors. Just coming onto the edge of the harbour was a frog-man. He was wearing a long, greenish cloak which dragged beneath his feet. Indeed, the cloak seemed to be getting right under his feet, which were well hidden by the folds. Perhaps the creature was injured. She suspected this, not because of any visible injury, but because his hopping motion was laboured, forced and distinctly off rhythm. His eyes seemed fixed and were certainly missing the normal gleam. The rest of his body was covered by the cloak, making a full diagnosis of his skin condition unachievable.

One of the frog-men started shouting at the newcomer. At least, Calandra thought it was shouting. The cloaked frog-man didn't answer but continued his unsteady advance. One of her captors leaped in front of the lurching figure, arms waving furiously, then dropped like a stone to the ground. Calandra saw the arrow lodged deep in his forehead, right between the eyes. The green cloak exploded open and two swift arrows raced into the heads of the two fish-men, before a third whirled its way towards the second frog-man. The smallest of warnings was enough for him to leap high into the air, avoiding a deadly bolt to the temple, unlike his fellow amphibians.

The cloak had dropped from the mystery frog-man's shoulders, revealing black-clad legs and a torso sporting a quiver strap. The figure, with the bow still in his right hand, clasped its lips and tried to pull top and bottom apart. This was interrupted by the remaining frog-man landing directly in front of the imposter and launching himself head first into his opponent's body. Both figures tumbled to the ground with the attacker slipping off the side of the harbour into the churning surf below.

An unforgettable roar drew Calandra's attention back to the water, a roar alien in concept and delivered from under the sea. Tentacles were now surfacing along with the protruding head, and from their proximity, Calandra knew she would soon feel their touch. Watching in horror, she saw one dark tentacle rip out from the sea towards her, stretching for her body. At the same moment, the pole she was suspended from swung away from the harbour. The tentacle missed her body by inches as she underwent a forced rotation, but it managed to latch some suckers on to her jacket. The jacket was ripped backwards, and for a moment she was caught with her feet tied to the mooring and her jacket held by the sea creature.

The pole had been rotated by the impostor and, still holding it, he was suddenly lifted off his feet as the tentacle started to pull back. He saw Calandra's jacket being yanked back to the sea, and Calandra with it, legs still tied tight. Finally, the jacket ripped hard around her hands, shredding the binds from her wrists so that she was hanging freely. The imposter drew an arrow and fired, slicing the rope holding her feet. Calandra fell to the ground but managed to force out her arms to break her fall.

Running to meet her, the imposter threw her over his shoulder and started to run away from the water's edge. Before four steps had been taken, a figure landed squarely in front of them. It was the other frog-man, and he stood braced to leap at them both.

Two tentacles raced out of the water, one grabbing the frog-man and pulling him directly into the water. The other wrapped itself round the head of the imposter and whipped him off his feet, causing him to drop his bow and Calandra in the process.

Calandra could see him being dragged back to the sea, racing across the cobbles of the harbour floor. He clattered into the upright post of the pole that had supported Calandra's weight, stretched his hands out and wrapped them around it. The tentacle continued to pull, and the frog's head deformed as it elongated. Then there was a drastic sucking sound coupled with a muffled human yell, and the head was hauled off into the watery depths.

The remaining human figure turned quickly, half stumbling, half running toward Calandra before grabbing the bow with his left hand and Calandra's T-shirt with his right. With urgency but extreme clumsiness, he dragged her off into the snow-covered dunes.

Once well clear of the harbour, the man collapsed onto the ground. Calandra lay on her back, breathing hard, contemplating the fate she had avoided. Her arms felt like they had been ripped from their sockets, so she was pleased to find she could reach her gag and remove it. Slowly, checking each limb, she reached down to her feet and undid the ties. Standing up, she felt a little off balance but was able to reach down to her saviour and tap his back. A brief moan was the reply.

"Hey, thanks. You handle that bow nearly as well as a friend of mine." She reached down and rolled the man over.

"I am never making pumpkin lanterns at Halloween again!" Kirkgordon responded.

Calandra bent down to kiss him hard but recoiled at the blood, innards and possible brain matter covering his face. Taking some snow, she washed his face as best she could before kissing him deeply and tenderly on the lips.

Kirkgordon looked up at the Russian beauty kneeling over him. For a moment he nearly responded to the longing in her kiss, to its thankfulness, its desire to show appreciation. But then he thought of the one she reminded him of.

"Don't let my wife catch you doing that," Kirkgordon laughed. The tension of the moment cracked and Calandra smiled.

"Your staff's by the path," he said, sitting up. The memory of cutting off and then gutting the frog-man's head flooded back to him. Never again, thought Kirkgordon. Next time she's fish food. But he knew he didn't mean it.

Calandra returned and stood before him, leaning on her staff, white wisps of snow slowly wetting her top and trousers, the wind whipping against her.

Good job she's ice, thought Kirkgordon. "Better get going, Cally. I'm starting to go numb." She threw out a hand to help him up. Gratefully he took it before pointing back down the sand dune path.

"That way. I've marked it."

"Churchy, why did you come for me? Havers would have told you to protect Indy. Indy's important. He has to do the right thing. You need to make sure."

"Havers is a pro. It's all about the mission. Everything calculated. And yes, he's right, Indy does need watching."

"So why? Don't get me wrong, Churchy, but if we lose the world it's a pretty poor exchange."

Kirkgordon laughed. "When he calls me

Churchy, Austerley's not having a pop at me, Cally. It's the difference between us. He examines everything, wants to understand it and control it. Whereas I have trust that when I wade in, there's someone watching over."

"I'm not sure I get it."

"No, it's easy," chuckled Kirkgordon. "Havers and you need a little faith."

"I've seen too many bodies over the years to have that."

"Then the coldness is in the heart, not the flesh. No man's gonna change that for you. But we have hope. Austerley may prevail."

"I've known him for twenty years. He's intoxicated with this stuff, anything strange. This is a fool's hope."

"Maybe. Probably more like an idiot's hope. But Austerley is the means. I have faith in God, and God says to have faith in Austerley."

"You may see that tested yet. Come on."

Chapter 25

How We See Things

Austerley was in his element. Escorted by creatures not normally seen on the surface of this world, being lauded as the one who would now bring forth Master Dagon; the respect shown for his intellect counteracted the poor figure he cut tramping through the snow. His bruised and battered face took on a ridiculous slant when his nose turned Rudolph-like with the incessant cold. Flakes of snow hung from wiry eyebrows, and tiredness slumped his shoulders. A majestic master of ceremonies he wasn't.

Yet the excitement was bubbling in his veins at the thought of meeting an Elder. For years, he had studied these alien creatures' rule on earth, stunning even the faculty at Miskatonic University. Of course, they wouldn't let him loose on the students; such young minds were not ready for such knowledge. Better that wiser men, like himself, should be carrying the mantle for the human race.

One thing was bothering him. Would they have all the elements necessary for the summoning? Fools thought it was like calling a dog forth from its kennel, but this was no resurrection of a frightening "Mary Rose". There would be the portal to open, deep beneath the surface, establishing the connection to the furthest reaches of space. Then the tribute to lay before the creature, drawing him forward into the continuum, causing him to appear deep beneath the surface and then to rise triumphant.

That was the real sticking point. How could he summon Dagon and then send him back? Once unleashed, there was no telling what devastation the Elder would bring. It wasn't like the book gave you a spell to put the genie back in the bottle. And Kirkgordon would be out of his depth with this. As would Havers. Calandra would see a real man dealing with the wilder things of this existence.

Their time together had been fun. In and out of the Russian social scene, albeit the darker and stranger end of it. She had introduced him to so many characters kept out of the everyday light for fear of upsetting the average person. For fear of unleashing the mob. In the back cafés and underground rooms they had been a perfect pair, her resplendent in her cold, perfect frame, and him with a brain to appreciate it.

Kirkgordon didn't know her, didn't really see the wonder of her. A curse, he saw a curse. But she was perfection.

The march from the house to the uncommunicated destination was taking a long time. Thoughts of sore feet and cold limbs broke into Austerley's mind and he started to complain at his escorts.

"I guess those flipper-feet don't feel the cold. Not much thickness to them, I guess. Damn slow walking though. What do you say, Kermit?"

Kermit said nothing. Fairly inarticulate really, thought Austerley. I was expecting a higher level of development. They don't seem up to much more than guard duty. All those years in space, travel amongst worlds, and what do they do? Drink, eat fish, worship some watery deity and pitch up for guard duty. Dagon better have more than this. Their path took them past a residential property on its own by a cliff edge. The frog-men ushered Austerley over to the front door of the house, which was lying slightly ajar. The fish-men with them split and circumnavigated the house before returning to the front. Satisfied of their solitude, the fish-men joined the others inside. Spying a door toward the rear of the hall which could serve only a smallish room, Austerley opened it to find a toilet and wash basin. He tried to shut the door behind him but a flipper was lodged between the door and its frame.

Normally, "passing the solids", as his mother had put it, was a time of thoughtful contemplation to Austerley; hidden away, secure and, in the most direct sense, occupied. However, it was hard enough to poo, never mind dream up plans for defeating an Elder, with a six-foot frog watching your every movement. The thought made him laugh, his first, he realized, in a long while.

After cleaning up, Austerley was led into the front room. Like most living rooms, it had a television in one corner, with surround sound, Austerley noted. There was a long sofa against the back wall and a table was set before the large window, looking out to the wildness where they had been walking. A dim uplighter barely raised the light level above an autumn morning's gloom, but it was clear that beyond the fish-men, some people were sitting on the sofa.

On the left was a man dressed in blue corduroy trousers and a pale green shirt. His close-cropped black hair and thick-set jaw complemented a rugged body. In his right hand was a tin of lager, opened and slightly crushed into his hand. The smile that adorned his face had the macabre relish of a fiend. But it was the gash across the neck, with its dark brown bloodstain, that drew up the bile from Austerley's stomach.

A quick glance showed the rest of the family in a similar situation on the right of the sofa. Austerley turned his back and vomited profusely onto the dark, thick carpet. The fish-man next to him made some comment in their language followed by what seemed to be a laugh. On his knees, with eyes streaming tears and remnants of sick dripping down onto his jacket from his chin, Austerley was surprised to find a can of the same lager thrust in front of his face.

"Bastards!" he shouted, pushing the can away and rising up to his feet. Half stumbling, half running, he raced out of the living room, staggered down the hall and tripped out of the front door, tumbling into the snow. Austerley clutched some snow together and hurled it at the window in a pathetic show of anger. The amphibians raised their cans to him, presumably laughing. He scrabbled around in the snow and found a rock.

"Bastards!" The front window shattered with the impact. It wasn't that he felt any better, just that he believed he had registered some note of protest. Ineffectual, certainly, but not unheard. All thoughts of higher forms of life had left Austerley's mind and been replaced with visions of totalitarian regimes and dictatorships. Even Russia had never gotten like this.

Sitting up on his knees, he allowed the wind to freshen up his face. After a minute he wiped the remaining drools of sick from his lips and chin, using a little snow to wash his face. Nothing was taking the gut- wrenching feeling in his stomach away. Nothing.

How many, wondered Austerley, how many? People who had lived here, had their ancestors here, grandparents and parents reared on this island. Now just removed. In fact, not even just removed, but butchered and then mocked. In tableau. It wasn't human. Wasn't that the point? Dagon, all this time he had been thinking of Dagon. The Philistines had worshipped him, but back then he hadn't showed up. He was just a statue to them, an image. They hadn't known the real thing. And Churchy, with his God, his meek and mild Jesus. How could he accept this?

Did all these things in shades of darkness bring such destruction? Carter, Pickman? Weren't they just adventurers like him, seeking the unknown, the galactic truth? Calandra, wasn't she an angel of good?

His world spinning towards an intellectual oblivion, Austerley just stared out at the cold night, watching the snow cover all in a pure unspoilt white. He wished that life could be so easily restored.

Scanning the surroundings, he hoped to catch a glimpse of Kirkgordon or maybe Calandra with her staff. He needed a rescuer. A whirlwind saviour to blow away the amphibians behind him and speed him away to a happiness clear of this dilemma he faced. If he refused to cooperate, he would be sat on the couch with a tinnie in his hand. If he went along with what they wanted, then he would betray his own race, unleashing hell from beneath the ocean floor. Worst of all, if he took it to the point of summoning before backing out, they would no doubt tear him limb from limb.

Never before had he needed courage, only curiosity. The cat-like desire had driven him into such dangerous and bleak situations. Now there was no desire except to be away from here. Looking inside, he saw his courage had failed. Fear started to become a reality, stronger than any desire he had ever felt.

In the asylum, there had been days like this after the incident in the graveyard. He remembered mooching around in a sloth of despair from having seen the dreaded things deep beneath that tombstone. Night after night, Austerley was rescued from their clutches by a gun-toting Kirkgordon only to resurface at the same tombstone and have a hysterical Kirkgordon leer over him. Kirkgordon's body had turned black, with large wings extended, his face twisted, eyes shimmering red.

The drugs had helped. He had been grateful for them, especially the happy ones. Even the naked dancing at the main street window, waving a towel above his head, shouting "Olé!" and impressing the rather elderly pair of women out for a Sunday walk had been worth it. But there were no drugs now.

Austerley looked around and saw the cliff edge behind the house. Rising to his feet, he turned slowly and quietly, stepping furtively towards the precipice. He reached the edge undetected and stood contemplating the drop below. It was a hundred-foot drop to the first rocks beneath. Austerley watched the waves crash hard into the impertinent fixture, breaking on impact, retreating to regroup again. This was perfect. At last he could see the way out. By throwing himself to this present doom he would evade all they had planned for him and not sell out his own race in the process.

Arms raised, Austerley let himself fall forward,

imagining himself leaving the ski jump, gliding to the foot of the hill. The air left a deposit of salt spray on his face and that, combined with the cold nip, made him feel more alive just as he exited this world. Austerley had found his peace.

It was like the fairground ride that catapults you suddenly several hundred feet into the air. Except that you had been blindfolded and not been told what you were being strapped into. In fact, you didn't even realize you were strapped into anything.

Austerley felt a pressure around his waist and was taken along a perpendicular plane at great speed over the sea. Then, almost rebounding, he was thrust back along his previous descent, and the grip on him was released. He cleared the cliff edge by ten feet before crashing and then sliding in the snow. His eyes, only then opening, saw the tentacle disappear back down towards the sea.

On his back, winded and badly bruised, Austerley cursed how his attempted death had turned into another of life's screw-ups. A shadow caught the top of his eye and he tilted his head back to see a familiar face.

"Careful now, Mr Austerley, we can't have our master of ceremonies being absent on our opening night."

Austerley shook his head in disbelief.

"You can piss right off, Farthington!"

Chapter 26

Back on the Old Job

"How high can you fly, Cally?" asked Kirkgordon.

"Not very. They're more for manoeuvring than for height or sustained flight. Useful for attacking people though."

"So you can't get some height up and see if you can spot Austerley?"

"Well, certainly not in this wind. I would probably be spotted, too. They are noticeably large. I thought you'd left a marker anyway."

"I did. But this snow is coming down awful thick. Could be difficult to track."

They continued jogging hard, side by side, along the dune path until Kirkgordon spotted the stick he had left behind.

"We're in luck. That way, Cally, but we'll need to be quick. Those footprints are just about discernible."

"What footprints? I can't see anything."

"Trust me. That way."

Calandra thought they seemed to be cutting across random fields with occasional nondescript broken bits of wall. Often, the wall was barely indistinguishable due to the snow piled high against its side. There was a distinct lack of trees and the terrain consisted of ridges – long thick cuts through the surface producing drops and climbs of several feet.

"Where did these come from? Seems unnatural. Do you think they were searching for something?"

"No, Cally. These are peat banks. They cut the turf off and then slice up the sod before drying it. Burn it in their houses. Flavour their whisky with it."

"Feels alien! I thought it was gas and oil fields out here, anyway."

"This is old school. Tradition that keeps going but you're right, they're bloody hard on your knees when you're tracking."

Continuing on in silence, Kirkgordon kept his scan going as he breathed in rhythm with his pounding feet. Something up ahead caught his eye. Grabbing Calandra by the scruff of her top, he dived into the snow, taking her down with him.

Slowly, he looked up to see approximately twenty creatures parading along the track ahead, a mixture of frog-men and fish-men. Many carried what Kirkgordon believed to be instrument cases. One looked similar to a fiddle case, another a guitar, a larger one like a double bass and several were small boxes perhaps containing flutes or clarinets.

"It's the band, Cally."

"Certainly appears to be. Want to take them out? They may be an important bit of the ceremony."

"Maybe they are, but twenty of them against us? We had enough trouble with just that one. No, we'll trail these guys. To be honest, I've been guessing at the trail this last two miles, so this is a better bet. They're bound to be going to the main event, so I reckon we follow. Otherwise Austerley's on his own."

The pace of pursuit slowed as the pair trailed the bizarre company at a distance. With fewer energies expended, Kirkgordon's mind drifted back to Havers' last words about Austerley.

For all his bluster about having faith in Indy, there was a deep doubt in the back of his mind. He's such a kid around these things, thought Kirkgordon, never seeing the disaster just round the corner. Kirkgordon had no doubt Dagon could be stopped, but whether Austerley was the man to do it seemed questionable. It had pepped Cally up, giving her a confidence in Indy.

Still, if Austerley buckled, Kirkgordon would need to deliver the killing blow. Despatching these amphibian abominations was one thing, but he had always done protection detail – he had on occasion shot in self-defence but never as an assassin. But wasn't this self-defence? Defence of the entire human race. Dear God, don't let it come down to a choice. Let him do the right thing. But You never force, do You? His own words rang hollow in his ears. Have a little faith.

"Is this Dagon real?"

The question totally blindsided Kirkgordon and all he could respond with was "What?"

"I've seen plenty but this is a new one on me. Dagon, is it like a real god? A real beast? What is it? Do we even know if this summoning will work?" As she was keeping low, Calandra struggled to see Kirkgordon's face, to read the truth of his reaction.

"Austerley thinks it's some sort of portal to a different part of space. Whether it is, or whether it's a road to hell, or even just a mad bluff, who knows? But I have been down in the depths with creatures that surely weren't holy, with black winged beings that nearly took my life, and with frog-men and fish-men. Whatever they really are, or wherever they have come from, they seem to be evil. They bring chaos and destruction, and their constant desire to rip me apart is having a really negative effect on their popularity rating."

"And what of me? Am I unknown to you? Do I seem unholy?"

"Whatever cursed you, Cally, scarred you deep. This coldness that affects your body, it changes you, too. You doubt yourself around people, you use your sexuality to compensate, because you think men see you as a freak, a curiosity. No doubt some do."

"Most are scared of my touch."

"Yes. That's the point. No closeness. No shared burden. Your curse dominates what you are. Even when you try to get past it, it still drives people's reactions, including your own. It does need to go, Cally."

"I just want to be normal again. To be free to express myself to people, not to hide. Not to have to compensate always."

"Then it has to be lifted. It must go away. Otherwise whatever you do, they will always see it. Don't misunderstand me – you are precious. You've saved me many times. And you are worth it. I can't change this bind you have, but I'll help. When this is done, we'll find a way."

"You truly believe that? I can be free of this curse?"

"Yes. Look for the good, always. If I don't, I lose any hope for Austerley." And hope is all I have, he thought. Come through for me, oh dear God, come through, cos I'm out of my depth.

He had been fighting with strange amphibians, a twelve-year-old boy had had to kill for him, he was looking at a kamikaze flight in a microlight through a severe snow storm and there was a strong possibility that the world would end, but he had to admit it: right at this moment, Havers was enjoying himself.

Back in his engineering days, before the call to stand up for his country in a more clandestine role, engines were his thing. Enrolled as an engineer in the RAF, he had served his time maintaining so many aircraft. And now it was flooding back to him.

The microlight hadn't been used in at least a month but it was in good condition. It was just a matter of making sure everything was turning and reconnecting the major parts. It was so simple, so clean and easy. Well, technically. He was splattered in oil and muck and his brain was spinning through the checks he needed to do. He may have been in a hurry but there was no way he was dropping into the sea twenty minutes after take-off.

The activity was helping the child too. James was understandably in shock from his actions, but Havers' cool, methodical chatter calmed him. The previous fascination James had shown in happy times was starting to come through and Havers was happy to engage with him.

"A twist of that. There! That should be us done on the engine. Time to get the wing on once I give her a quick turn. Oh, and let's see what fuel we have, James. See who's going to get on board."

James scurried off round the room, turning over everything. The jerrycans were already accounted for but Havers doubted they would be enough to carry them both to the mainland. Opening the apparently full can, Havers instantly swore, recognizing the smell of diesel.

"What is it?" a worried James asked.

"Diesel. It's no use for the plane. It must have been for his car."

"Are we stuffed then, Mister?"

"For the mainland, yes. But not for getting airborne round here, young James. We need to think differently, though. No point flying about if we cannot contribute to the party. I think we need to check the shelves and tins. Let's see if we can make a bang."

It took a while to catalogue all the substances before Havers decided how to combine them. There wasn't a lot, and anything heavy would weigh down the plane. Trying not to show his disappointment, Havers showed James how the wing was to be attached. James was very interested, though, and insisted on knowing the plans for the things that go bang.

"Well, it's not that simple, James. As I see it, with the things we have, there's no way to store any substances together without them going bang here on the ground or up there as we mix them. The only option is to drop the diesel and then set fire to it."

"Will that make a big bang?"

"No, but it should catch fire. We'll have to be fairly low if we're going to be accurate. And we need some way to light it. Check for rags and sticks."

James came back with a multitude of rags which had been thrown in a corner after they had become too soaked in oil or smeared in grime. The only sticks to hand were in a bag of kindling, long forgotten at the rear of the building. They seemed damp, which Havers thought a fortunate point, as the sticks were very short and wouldn't show much of a handle beneath a tied cloth.

Together they sat, wrapping rag after rag onto the short sticks then packing them inside some plastic bags which had been abandoned in a corner. The conversation dwindled as the time to execute their mission drew closer.

"James, you don't need to come with me. You can stay here and lay low, or you could return to your mother. I will not lie to you, son, there's no safe option. It will be difficult to just keep myself alive, I cannot guarantee you will be safe with me. But it's your choice."

James looked at Havers, then stared at the ground, silent. He's too young for this, thought Havers. And I'm too old.

"Can I go with you, Mr Havers?"

"Of course, James."

"If I go back to Mum I might lead some of them to her. I don't want to be on my own. So I reckon helping you is the thing to do. If that's okay. I'll do whatever you need done."

"It's just fine, James. You're a brave lad. I think your dad would be proud." Actually, thought Havers, your dad would ask me what the hell I was thinking taking his son into an apocalyptic nightmare. But as he's not here and I need the help, stuff it.

After opening the doors of the building, together they pushed the body of the microlight out of the door into the deepening snow. Next, they packed the rag-topped kindling and the diesel jerrycan. The wing was the hardest piece of the jigsaw to assemble; they had to fight hard to extract it from the room and fix it onto the body of the microlight.

Havers held the wing tight with one hand while he started up the engine. As soon as the fan kicked into life, he jumped into the cockpit and signalled James to join him. Turning slowly into the wind, Havers sought a straight and even run for departure.

"Good luck, James," roared Havers over the engine. The child didn't speak but fixed his eyes ahead. Here goes nothing, thought Havers, and the tiny aircraft sped quickly down the improvised runway before leaving the snowy ground behind.

Chapter 27

Captive Desires

Austerley remembered the needle they put in his arm, the sharp stab of pain when they found the vein and the continued dull annoyance while the fluid was injected. And then sleep. A strange sleep with no dreams. Then the slap across his cheek.

"Wake up, Mr Austerley! Time to wake up and listen. The situation is very perilous, Mr Austerley. A friend of yours is in trouble. She was stupid enough to follow you and now she's in the room with us. You can see her, Mr Austerley. Sat across from you. Look at her."

Austerley's eyes could perceive only blurred scatterings of light with no definition. The light was so damn bright in his face. Squinting hard, he could just make out a shape he recognized. Farthington! Bastard. There were some other indistinct shapes. Goons, thought Austerley. And over there, in the corner... no, no, no! Kirkgordon must have abandoned her. Sweet Calandra.

"Ah, so you see her, Mr Austerley. You recognize her, of course."

"It's Calandra. Let her go!"

"So you see her trouble, then?"

Austerley was tipping toward rage, restrained only by the hope of seeing a way out of this mess. Calandra had her arms tied up high above her head. Her bare feet were just about touching the floor; he couldn't tell whether she was hanging on her restraints or supporting her weight from beneath. Her long hair flowed down her back on to a ripped white crop top. With only a white thong, her smooth legs were visibly taut. A pair of strong black wings set off her pale flesh. Even in bondage she looks magnificent, thought Austerley.

"You could at least show her some dignity. Displaying her womanhood to all this filth!"

These drugs are damn good, thought Farthington, and let out a smug chuckle.

"You sick bugger," Austerley continued. "She's a thing of wonder. Not for your dirty hands."

"Ah, yes. My hands. Well, Mr Austerley, I was wondering if you would oblige me in some trouble I am having with a little ceremony we are undertaking. Otherwise, I may just have to get my hands dirty with something else."

"Get your hands off her! And cover her up again!

Touch her with your mouth in that way again and I'll never help you."

Farthington watched Austerley stare at the empty corner, revulsion on his face.

"Maybe she'll like this," said Farthington. "With practice, she'll learn to."

"Stop! Stop it! Leave her alone!" Tears were starting to stream, clouding Austerley's eyes again. "Cut her down. Cover her. I'll do what you want. Dammit, I'll do it. Just leave her alone. Don't spoil her."

"Cut her down and cover her with that blanket!" announced Farthington. Four frog-men looked blankly at him. "Remember I still have her, Mr Austerley, and I can uncover her any time I choose."

"Don't touch her again. Just don't."

"Well that's up to you, Mr Austerley. You know what it is I want. Ever since our little tête-à-tête in Russia you have known, deep down in the recesses of your mind. Dagon shall rise and rule this world. And for my service and worship, I shall rule Russia for him, Mr Austerley. Dear old Mother Russia will be mine."

"Dagon? You seriously believe Dagon will give a damn about you? The moment he rises he will wreak havoc and destruction on everyone. He will acknowledge no favours, no rule except his. This is your death sentence too."

"Let's say I have a little more faith in our beings from afar than you do, Mr Austerley. We all want worship, after all."

"He is the lack of order, he is chaos. Don't do this."

Farthington addressed the frog-men. "Get Mr Austerley to his feet and show him to his changing room." As they sprang into action, he turned back to Austerley. "As the one to minister the opening of the passage you need to be accurately dressed. We both know it's more than symbolism. Smile, Mr Austerley, you are harbouring in a new dawn for humanity."

The frog-men took Austerley by the arms and half led, half dragged him to a small room. Having been delivered and most certainly deposited into the room, Austerley took a moment to get his bearings. There was a sink with a mirror above and a small door leading to a toilet. Otherwise, the only item in the room was a portable clothes rail on which several garments were hanging.

Realizing this was his outfit for the ceremony, Austerley decided to see if it fitted. He took a long white tunic and forced his head through the smallish opening. On ruffling the item down his body, he found it to be particularly tight around the waist. There were some bizarrely pointed shoes, which pinched his toes, and a decorative belt with plenty of holes for fastening but none allowing it to fit around his waist. It took a while to make a new hole with the pin of the belt. He remembered that the man whom Havers had ejected from the window was of a smaller frame.

"That's because he wasn't a real man."

Austerley spun round to see Calandra standing

just inside the door, covered in the blanket Farthington had given her.

"How did you get away?"

"I had to see you. I needed one moment alone with the only man I could ever want. You're my hero and you deserve your send-off. One last fling with your Countess, one last perfect union."

Austerley gulped as Calandra dropped the blanket, revealing every piece of ice-cold glory. His pulse raced and his breathing quickened as every hope and memory came home. Calandra had become the prize on his arm, full of wanton passion for her true admirer, the one who could appreciate her best. As she came close, he felt the adrenalin surge.

"What happened here? Why's he not ready?"

Farthington understood the language of the frog-men and fish-men, up to a point. Still, he had his doubts. Apparently, Austerley had just collapsed, hitting the floor in a spectacularly loud crash which had alerted the guards. No one had gone in or out, but Austerley, on waking, had been looking for a naked woman. Maybe the drugs are too good, thought Farthington, but it's too late to back out now.

"Get him into the outfit, now! We have a schedule to meet."

Austerley was frogmarched from the room five minutes later, stumbling in his new garb. On top of the white tunic were draped two scarf-like pieces of black material displaying all sorts of occultic signs.

Austerley recognized them quite clearly from the Necronomicon and knew the significance they held. He was to be the attraction, the bait to draw Dagon through the continuum The first one to look into those eyes of blackness, and doubtless only madness lay beyond. The machinations of the corrupted beings around him had skewed his view from the curious to the outright horrified.

Farthington looked down at the black socks and boots visible beneath the inadequate tunic. Marsh had certainly been a smaller man.

"Remember we still have her. Anything not in line with the ceremony, Mr Austerley, and she will have to be terminated. Pity, such a wonder and so very beautiful with it."

"Leave her alone, Farthington. You'll have your hell!"

Turning on his heel, Farthington led the small party out of the building. Austerley was accompanied on either side by two hopping frog-men. The repetitive splodges of their landings irritated Austerley to such a degree he started thinking about performing transplants on them to give them back their once-human legs. He had heard the tales of the Innsmouth folk, but the reality was too gross.

Leaving the dank, grey building by the front door, the small party proceeded down a small avenue of gorse bushes before emerging into a great expanse. The sea was visible on all sides, and the wild grass at Austerley's feet, poking out like the sole survivor through the snowfall, ran up to the edge of a cliff. The cliff was horseshoe in shape and approximately a quarter of a mile wide, with the over-emphasized tips of the horseshoe pointing at each other. The drop down was only some hundred feet but it was sheer. All along the cliff were amphibians, some with instruments, some with staffs and tiaras, but all dressed in colours once bright and gaudy but which now looked like over-washed hand-me-downs.

With Farthington in the lead, Austerley trudged behind feeling like an escaped mental patient in his ill-fitting clothing. From his studies he recognized everything around him, but he now saw it through a different lens. Horror had truly found its place in his mind. No longer did he see misunderstood beings with superior intellect. Rather, he saw the drive for power and the merciless removal of all standing in the way. Neither was he immune to seeing this as a human trait, one brought on this world by these degenerate spawn of Innsmouth.

They stared at him as he approached the centre of the cliff-side. Not with the evil eyes from the pub, but now with hope. The trepidation and excitement of the creatures was infectious, and he was starting to tense up. Snow continued to fall and he felt he was in a black Christmas celebration. The elements were all there: bunting, tinsel, decorative signs and symbols; but all were torn or worn down, devoid of their birthday colours.

At the centre of the horseshoe there an immense diving board. Yes, thought Austerley, like the ones the cliff-divers use, wide and sturdy with no flex whatsoever. Except this was no sporting apparatus but rather a stage.

"There is your marker, Mr Austerley," said Farthington, "a prime platform with which to welcome our new master. Follow me."

Austerley walked out onto the platform with Farthington and immediately felt dizzy at the height of it. A strong wind was blowing; he felt the need to stay in the middle of the board, giving himself some five feet on either side.

"As you can see, Mr Austerley, we have quite a gathering today. From wide and far they have come to celebrate with us. Your name will be held high for years to come as the one who opened the gateway. I suggest you get past your moral difficulties and embrace it!"

Austerley looked gingerly beyond the board out to sea. There were things out in the sea. Dark shadows there hinted of a tentacle or an arm. Maybe a flipper, possibly sharp teeth and slimy backs. The perversion of the sea was before him.

"Nearly show time, Mr Austerley. I suggest we retire back to the cliff-side and proffer you a cup of tea. We don't want those vocal chords failing on a night like this."

"There's Indy!"

"Okay Cally, stay down. It's not going to be easy to get close to him. Especially at the moment. There's nothing to draw anyone's attention."

"Can you hit from this distance?"

"In this wind? Not a chance."

"What if we took out a couple of frog-men and..."

"There's no way I am sticking my head back up in one of those again. For flips' sake, Cally. It's not anything I want to think about."

"So how do we get closer, then?"

"There are humans about too. Have a look for some with clothing that hides the face. Anything with a hood."

"Okay." Searching the night, they found the dark shapes too indistinct until a sudden revelation of the moon brought them luck.

"There, Churchy! By that building. Looks like the toilet block."

"Good, time to move. I don't see it being long if they have Austerley here already."

Chapter 28

Stars From the Deep

Two black figures were not seen disappearing into the gentlemen's toilets. Neither were they heard dropping onto the tiled floor of the urine-smelly facilities. Two figures then walked out dressed in brown robes with large cowls covering their heads. Emblazoned on the robes were marks associated with Dagon and his order, but the only thing that was bothering one of the figures was the smallness of the shoulders.

"Damn it, Cally. If I open up with my arrows in this, the back's gonna rip apart."

"Are you sure the stomach fits?" Calandra was teasing and he knew it. She's nervous, thought Kirkgordon, probably more like petrified underneath. Probably best to find a gap somewhere with not many about and prepare for the show. The closer the better, though. It's going to be hard to hit Austerley in this wind. If I have to. Please God, make that a no!

Figures were gathering along the cliff-edge, three to four deep in places. Kirkgordon and Calandra walked along the rear of the crowd, eventually coming to the tip of an encompassing arm on the south side. The view of the platform in the middle of the natural arena was quite clear as the crowd was more dispersed here.

"Okay. Will this do?"

"Tough shot, but yes. Not much of an escape route, though, for when we have to get out."

"I doubt we'll need one, Churchy. I think this is a last stand whatever happens," she whispered into his cowl.

He nodded. Before his mind's eye flashed first his kids. The last they had known of him were the screaming nights, his churning mind and drained body, without sleep and covered in sweat. He hoped they could remember the times before, prayed that they weren't too young. And then Alana. They'd been so young when they'd first met, but she'd gripped him from the start. Every woman he'd seen since had only reminded him in some way of her. His unfaithful lapses formed a spiral that always came back to her. Surprisingly, he felt no pain at losing her but thankfulness for what had been. Here, facing the cold draught of an unbeatable evil, he instead tasted a warm summer beer. Familiar, fresh, wholesome and without compare.

The striking-up of music brought him back to his senses. On the far side of the arena, Kirkgordon could see a mass orchestra tuning up, producing dreadful tones. They were a mass of frog-men, fish-men, humans and other creatures he tried not to study too closely. Dilapidated music stands and folders, many inscribed with the legend EOD, littered the far side in a haphazard arrangement. Strings, brass, woodwind, percussion – all were being warmed up.

As if cued in by the orchestra, the crowd started to push closer to the edge to see the party who would mount the platform. The surge was so great that a few creatures fell forward off the cliff, down toward a fate that was beyond Kirkgordon's sight. A buzz of babbling and croaking rose up. Here we go, thought Kirkgordon, and he gently touched the edge of his habit, feeling for the solid line of his concealed bow.

Austerley nervously drank some of the tea offered to him. It tasted like it had come from an urinal, but then the water round here must be polluted, with this scum running the show. In the distance he could hear the orchestra starting up, each instrument running over their little piece from Zahn's music, one more key in the calling forth of Dagon.

He had often wondered where Zahn had got the manuscript from, since it was clearly not his own composition. What being from far-off worlds had, at one time, come to that street? Why had Zahn taken up rooms there? Why had he never run? Austerley knew why. That same burning intrigue that had hooked Austerley for so long, until the real vision of these "better" creatures could be seen.

"The time is upon us, Mr Austerley. If you would kindly step forward and take up the elements of calling forth. And remember, I have her close if anything goes wrong."

Held by the wrist, Calandra was huddling her blanket around her, occasionally struggling against Farthington's strong hold. Tears welled in Austerley's eyes and he tried to focus as a small bag was placed in front of him.

Opening it, his eyes examined the items for the ceremony. All had on them old inscriptions in a language only a few living people knew. Austerley was one of these people and, although he chastened himself for being only the third-best authority, one of the others was a wraith. It mattered little. He knew the order, deciphered from a nearly forgotten text. He had read it in a cemetery high in the Andes, some ten years ago, yet such was his mental agility back then, he had committed it all to memory. A memory that had failed him until Farthington had extracted it from him. And on recovery from that mental abuse his mind had held on to the necessary details.

He watched Farthington lead Calandra ahead of him. She stared at him with her pale face, begging for release. There was no need, thought Austerley, for him to drag her around in that state of undress, modesty protected only by that tatty blanket. When this was done, he would make Farthington pay.

Farthington, on the other hand, was reasonably happy that preparations were just about complete. Despite Austerley's apparent romantic attachment to Farthington's frog-man bodyguard, he seemed to be ready for the ceremony. The music was starting to waft into the air. That lamentable, grotesque, off-rhythm sonata he had heard time and again in preparation would only require one more play. Yes, all was going according to plan even though they had been unable to locate Kirkgordon, the girl and that government man.

The small party stepped up to the edge of the large board and waited a moment. A hush descended over the watching mass of monstrosity. A single discord was sounded by a guitar-equivalent, followed by some off-key blaring from a number of loud trombones. Then silence. Farthington turned to Austerley, nodding to indicate he move forward into position.

What Austerley saw, however, was Farthington nod grimly and hold Calandra by the neck to indicate her fate if he did not proceed. Bastard, right to the end. I will destroy him, whatever happens.

Austerley walked onto the board and the watching horde cheered wildly, an array of croaking and babbling and violent splashing in the sea. Taking the bag with the objects for the ceremony, he removed them one by one to arrange them in a circle around him. Lifting his hands in the air, he cried out in a language unheard for over several thousand years. His voice was not his own, but deep and rasping, with a malevolence never before seen on his face.

"Churchy," whispered Calandra into his cowl, "is he okay? That's not him. Is he in control? Is that him doing this?"

"How the hell should I know? I mean, does any of this look normal?"

"So what do we do? How do we know?"

"We just ride with it. See what happens. But if you see a hundred-foot demon-god with wings, take it that it's going badly."

The orchestra was in full swing with its unholy cacophony of sound which grated at Austerley's nerves. He focused by throwing surreptitious glances towards the object of his affection. After first calling out to the far reaches, the ceremony proceeded to the creation of the portal. Into the sea were thrown three stones, each in order and according to their inscription, words that only Austerley could read.

There was movement beneath the board, as a whirlpool began in the water and a faint glow formed. As the water spun faster so the light grew stronger. The assembled mob started to dance and chant, forcing Kirkgordon and Calandra to join in lest they be discovered. The shrieks, jabberings and deep-throated croaks nearly split the ear drums, and Kirkgordon was reminded of a Middle Eastern funeral mob he had once been caught up in. The same wildness with unified purpose, common to all such gatherings. It had scared him, and even more so his protectee, but at least that mob had been human.

Austerley picked up a few of the small bags around him containing elements of a non-Terran nature. Of the five bags, he knew two of the elements well, having been able to collect them in the past. Pickman had always been a useful acquaintance. As for the other three, yes, he did know their names, but where they had been sourced he had not the least idea. They were things of legend, although the book had been very specific about their uses.

Standing on the edge of the board, he deposited the contents of the bags in the required order and watched the whirlpool below. The water frothed within the pool and the light changed from white to a deep blue. Slowly, there appeared small twinkling lights in the depths. One by one they appeared, in a variety of intensities, until the whole whirlpool had a night-sky backdrop. Austerley stared deep into the depths looking over every piece of the image. It was the sky map from the book.

The snow was still falling but it was melting about ten feet above the whirlpool. Steam was coming off the water and it started to obscure the previously brilliant image. Farthington stood on the edge, smiling, amazed at the power displayed beneath.

"Good, Mr Austerley. Now is the time. Fulfil the ancient book's tale of woe. Unleash the Master. Unleash him!"

Austerley, teeth gritted, stared at Farthington and

at the poor figure of Calandra beside him. She was crying, the blanket blowing in the hard wind, exposing her white flesh. Anger flowed through Austerley, coupled with frustration, and he grimly returned to his task.

Farthington wondered why Austerley was so fascinated, and indeed so angry, at the frog-man standing alongside. Ah, who cares, he thought. Another ten minutes and he could cast Austerley into the whirlpool.

There was a good view of the whirlpool from the south side. "Cally, do you recognize that sky?" shouted Kirkgordon over the hubbub.

"No. It's not from any galaxy that I've ever seen."

"Me neither. Cally, I think it's the portal!"

There were three pieces of rock remaining on the board. Each was about the size of a fist and singularly unimpressive. Yet they had cost so much to obtain. Farthington looked at his purchases being picked up by Austerley. One had cost a million and had been obtained without the US government's knowledge. The second had required an archaeological dig conducted at night, deep in the Andes. The last had required a visit to a grave Austerley was familiar with, one which had kept the rock's secret for over a thousand years. But it had been worth it. This was no megalomaniac's dream, this was a change in the order of things. This was the return of the gods of chaos, and Farthington was going to milk them for all they had to give. Every overseer requires a fixer. And fixers can make the rules.

One by one, Austerley dropped the rocks into the whirlpool. Each was greeted with a sharp explosion. Chanting long-forgotten and non-earthly incantations, Austerley stood on the edge with his hands outstretched, beckoning to the deep. He was one of the first to discern the shape.

Four triangular peaks were seen rising through the steam. They were spaced out but had a symmetry. As they started to rise, the outside peaks revealed jet black sheets beneath them. The central formations rested on a circular base.

"What the hell is that?" said Calandra.

"No idea, but it can't be good."

"Churchy, look! Eyes!"

Two red eyes were emerging, attached to the central base which was being revealed as a head. The outside sheets now showed talons on their edges. The half-head was already ten feet high and growing. A mouth with sharp fangs was revealed next. The gathering was in a frenzy.

"Austerley, no! No! Dammit! God preserve us! God help me!"

"Churchy, don't!"

Kirkgordon's robe was off and his bow drawn with an arrow aimed at the figure on the board.

"That's Dagon, Cally! That's your evil god rising. Austerley, you stupid shit!"

Chapter 29

To Kill an Austerley

With a lack of hesitation he found surprising, Kirkgordon let his arrow fly. In the wind and snow, the shot was a difficult one. Add to this the updraught from the whirlpool and Kirkgordon knew that if he hit the board it would be a good shot. As he watched the arrow arc down, his hopes were raised. It was in the vicinity.

Austerley was in full chanting mode, performing the final rites of passage that would allow the evil to break through to this world proper. The corner of his eye saw a shape coming at him from above. Instinctively, he leaned back. A screaming pain formed in his right foot but, knowing that any break now in his concentration would cause the whirlpool to collapse, he forced himself to ignore his foot and continue.

"Damn! It's too far to be accurate, Cally!"

"Never mind that," cried Calandra, dropping her habit and bringing her staff to bear on a nearby frog-man who had decided he was not amongst friends. "Just fire and I'll do what I can. They've clocked we're not fans!"

A pair of wings flashed out from Calandra's back and she raced into the crowd of frog-men beside them. The surprise of her attack meant she had laid several to the ground by the time they could rally. Using her wings for balance and ignoring her gammy leg, she spun her staff and gleaming white light emanated from its tips.

Kirkgordon didn't hesitate; another arrow was on its way.

Farthington had heard the thud from the arrow and was scanning the arena for its source. He grabbed the frog-man beside him and sheltered, peering from behind. The arrow came into view approximately half a second before impact and he ducked behind his guard. He heard the thud and his guard croaked a half-scream before toppling away from Farthington and off the board. Looking at the falling frog-man, Farthington could see the arrow deep in his neck.

Austerley was in pain, but it was something else that stopped his chant. Farthington had just dropped Calandra off the board into the whirlpool. He watched the blanket blow about in the wind as her

Crescendo!

naked form fell down towards Dagon himself.

"Farthington! I'll send you to hell!" Starting to chant a new phase, Austerley was wild with rage. His arms waved as he roared out his new song. Then the two menacing red eyes on the twenty-foot-wide head of the demon came into view. And it howled right in Austerley's face.

Austerley was brought back from his drug-induced dream into a dark, fearsome reality. He looked into the depths of evil, his mind spinning at the indescribable horror of the face of Dagon. Screaming aloud, he felt his mind being invaded with a force he had never known possible. It was like witnessing every possible inhuman act all at once. The gut-wrenching churning, the deep-seated terror, the chill running through every bone of your body, all of these and more. Sometimes he had wondered if he had a soul; now it was like it was being ripped apart deep in its core. Bile ripped up through his throat.

Farthington had turned his back on the rising demon and was racing to get off the board. As he brushed past Austerley, he was covered in a spew of vomit, but still he didn't stop. He could hear the rage of the creature and he was not going to be held responsible for it.

Austerley felt the taunting, the attack at his very being. His worthlessness was shown to him, his frailty was exposed, his every cowardly act that had ended in someone else's pain. Despair was grabbing hold of his mind. Seeing his doom, Austerley unleashed the mantra from the book, the one to close the door. Wailing it like a madman, he fought the terror that threatened to take his tongue, knowing failure would mean forfeiting his life, maybe even his essence. Where was Churchy's god when you needed him? Won't you help me? Or would you damn us all?

His tongue steadied. From nowhere, a force restored his nerve and he spoke the mantra now in fresh and constant tones. Gradually, he felt the black tentacles retreating from his mind, felt his senses coming off edge.

The demon in the whirlpool felt it too. That force once again. Dagon was toppling, to be laid out on the floor of its own temple. The great black wings started to thrash as it was struck with pain.

Calandra was being overpowered, several frog-men having hit her hard, and only her wings had shielded her from a fatal blow. Seeing her struggle, Kirkgordon joined the fray but the frog-men overwhelmed him and he was soon floored. On his back, slightly stunned, he suddenly felt himself cry out. Where are you, then? Come on, show me now. Or don't you care? I came, I did my bit. Why am I forsaken?

Dagon was descending back into the whirlpool but the demon's wings bore down on the sides of the arena, causing small avalanches of rock and sending amphibians into the deep. The orchestra music was cut short as the brass section, followed by the strings, toppled down the cliff into the maelstrom. Sea creatures were being drawn back into the whirlpool with tentacles waving and many fins struggling against the pull.

Kirkgordon rolled sideways as one of Dagon's massive wings crashed into the arena edge beside him. Several frog-men were instantly squashed flat, spraying slimy liquid over Kirkgordon and Calandra. The rock around them crumbled, dropping into the oceanic horror below. Several of the amphibians fell backwards from the ground shock and clattered into Calandra, making her stumble and tilt precariously over the edge. In that moment, Kirkgordon saw that she was not going to be able to remain on the high ground.

Calandra thrust her staff up above her as she descended through the air. Instinctively, Kirkgordon dived forward to snatch the weapon with his outstretched right hand. Although now in a horizontal position, he pulled up as hard as he could from his biceps but he feared the worst. The end of the staff soon emerged above the cliff-edge without its owner.

By now the whirlpool was sucking in deeply, like a mighty ogre drawing its breath. Kirkgordon, still on top of the dilapidated cliff, was suddenly caught up in the air flow and pulled over the edge. He tumbled down the smashed rocks, felt his left arm strike hard, breaking it, and then a hand grabbed his shirt. His right hand, still holding on to the staff, felt a colder hand slip over his and take the staff from him. The staff end, glowing an extreme white, whirled past him, drove into the remaining cliff face and buried itself deep within.

A pale arm curled itself round the staff.

Kirkgordon was slipping past it when a slender pair of legs hooked themselves around him and yanked him towards it. Grabbing the staff with his good right hand, he wrapped his legs and body round it. He felt a cold figure embrace him and clung on tight.

"Hold on, Churchy! Just hold!" Her hair whipped across his face as the staff began to bend.

Austerley also felt the draw of the closing continuum. The board was bending, and as it dipped down he could see Dagon all but disappearing back to his own place and time, wherever that was. But the board continued to bend as the wind was sucked down into the fracture. Something hit Austerley hard in the back. It was a man; he saw arms and then legs whip past his face. He watched his smart-suited former captor spin uncontrollably towards his doom. As frog-men and fish-men joined other amphibians in the whirlpool, Austerley saw Farthington change. First, wings emerged from his back. He grew three times his previous height and the suit fell away to be replaced by scales. Large nostrils and a protruded jaw with sharp teeth formed on each of three heads, and talons for feet completed the transformation.

The dragon fought hard against the river, flapping his wings and holding steady above the rapidly closing portal. He roared loudly, beating hard. Austerley was dragged closer to him as the board flexed further. Pivoting on the arrow jammed into his foot, Austerley was now hanging off the board, flailing head-first towards the continuum.

Then the board cracked. Austerley dropped. At once his mind seized the consequences. He was falling to the world of the very demon he had just sent back to its own realm. Dagon would have his revenge. The darkest of nights was upon him.

Chapter 30

Revenge of the Dragon

From his position on the bending staff, Kirkgordon had seen Farthington transform back into his natural form, fighting the pull of the continuum. He was then bemused to see Austerley, with a large piece of board attached to his foot, whizz past him, crashing into the water. He tried to follow Austerley into the water but Calandra held him tight to the staff.

"No, Churchy! No! It's too late!"

The whirlpool was starting to collapse, and Kirkgordon was able to glance around at the arena which had held the ceremony. There was no sign of the orchestra on the far side, only jagged rock formations. There were also no frog-men on his own side of the natural structure, all having been sucked deep into the continuum. After such a frenzy of noise, it was refreshing to have a relative silence, the crashing of the waves now seeming more natural with no tentacles or heads floating in the surf. His arm ached and he was breathing deeply in an endeavour to recapture the oxygen he had spent in self-preservation. His eyes stared grimly at the broken board.

Austerley was unaware of the worry focused on his previous position. Crashing into the sea upside down, his nostrils had filled with water and he had struggled not to swallow in panic. His foot was still attached to the board, which trailed behind him, stopping him from self-rectifying. Beneath him was the outlying vastness of Dagon's realm and a rapidly closing portal. His descent continued downwards until, approximately three metres from reaching the portal, it closed abruptly. As the body of water was forced to dissipate its momentum, Austerley was thrown about violently before drifting slowly toward the surface, pulled upward by the board. He had become numb to the pain of the arrow and indeed wondered if he could feel anything at all in his leg.

His progress to the surface was too slow and Austerley was out of breath. This is it, he thought. The thought brought him some relief, as he was sure he would no longer be spending time with Dagon, and surely Churchy's god, if that's where he was going, would be a lot more sympathetic. After all the turmoil, his only regret was not avenging

Calandra, not destroying Farthington for consigning Calandra to her doom. Yes, in a strange way, he was at peace. He was ready.

Calandra, seeing that the whirlpool had finished, let herself drop off the staff. Kirkgordon, counting on her support and not ready for this, dropped off too. He landed on his backside while Calandra touched down nimbly on her feet. She barely noticed as she watched the dragon, now free of any pull from the water, start to climb free. Without looking, her left hand grabbed her staff, pulling it clear of the rock.

"Cally! I'm fine, thanks for asking. Just bloody dandy."

"Shut up! Look! The dragon, look at him!"

"I see him. We need some cover. Somewhere to run to. Some..."

"Churchy, shush! Look at him. LOOK!"

"Yeah, he looks fine, now let's move."

"No, I said look! He's climbing up to circle. Churchy, he's looking for something."

"But it's all gone, Cally. Isn't it? I mean the water's no longer doing a washing machine. There's nothing down there. Nothing. The frog-men, fish-heads, sea creatures, they all got sucked in. There's bound to be the odd escapee, but basically the guts of them are gone."

The dragon circled high, flapping his wings with great frequency to effect a virtual hover over the last location of the now-defunct whirlpool. Then his eyes opened wide and snarls formed across his faces. All three heads looked toward a single point.

The dragon turned, then his body became almost arrow-like and dived into the water.

"He's diving, Churchy. He's seen something."

"There's nothing there, Cally. Except... Austerley?"

Having resigned himself to the oncoming darkness or light the crash of something entering the water shook Austerley's new utopia. He didn't care. What could matter now? Then suddenly he was no longer in the water.

The dragon had dived into the water like a sea eagle. Grabbing the board Austerley was attached to, he flew clear of the surface, his cargo dripping profusely. He climbed high, reaching some thousand feet before he turned and faced his passenger. One taloned foot remained clutching the board but the other gripped Austerley's body. Austerley let out a wild scream as the board was ripped off his foot. More accurately, his ankle broke, leaving his foot still attached to the board.

The dragon discarded the board and flew down to the snow-covered earth before dropping the rest of his cargo from a few feet. Austerley spun hard across the ground and then came to rest in the pure snow, colouring it a dark red. Setting down gently, the beast brooded over his motionless prize.

"Come on!" shouted Cally.

"I'm done, Cally. Go, go get him!"

Calandra scrabbled up the uneven rocks, her black wings helping her over the larger gaps. By the time she had cleared the top ledge of the cliff, her staff was already spinning and glowing white. She ran hard towards the beast, her weight lifting into her wings, making her quicker than her gammy leg would have allowed. Soon she was flying.

The dragon spoke. "Austerley! You... This was my prize. This was mine to have. Six years I have searched for the things this backward, ridiculous religion wanted. All the research, all the time expended. I even freed you from your padded walls, but no, you can't even manage a twenty minute presentation. That was all that was required. You useless excuse. You will pay for this. I will burn you to an inch of your life. Then I will take you apart limb by limb so that you cry out my name, wishing for death. You will beg, Austerley."

"It doesn't matter. You killed her. Why did you kill Calandra?"

The dragon was somewhat stunned by this response. Then comprehension dawned. Ah, the drugs, he thought. He was even more stunned by the incredibly hard staff that cracked down on to his middle skull. He roared and turned, unleashing a torrent of flame at his assailant. Calandra had continued over the top of the dragon and was on his opposite side when the hot fire was released. On the ground was a line of melted snow.

Calandra flew back over the head of the beast, causing him to spin round, heads thrashing wildly in a frustrated search for her. Realizing Calandra's trick, the dragon flew upward, crashing hard into Calandra, who fell to the snow. She looked up, awaiting the flame from its nostrils, but another sound filled the air.

"James, looks like we arrived late. See the dragon?"

"Yes, sir!"

"That's where I want the fuel dumped, on his heads. But be careful, because he'll fire back."

Farthington saw the microlight in the near distance and prepared to burn it out of the air. Gracefully lifting his large frame with his wings, he took in a large breath. As he waited those few precious seconds to get the microlight in his sights, he was struck hard on the back of his targeting head and felt a burning pain, like a drill overheating, boring into his skull. Calandra fell back to ground again, leaving behind her now half-buried staff.

Farthington thrashed around, desperately trying to remove the staff with his small arms, his other heads shaking crazily from the pain. Soon he realized that his arms were not going to provide a King Arthur moment. He lifted up one of his powerful legs, gripped the staff, ripped it out and flung it far away. As he did so, he smelt fuel and felt a liquid pour over his body. Looking up, he saw a boy hanging from the microlight with a flaming ragged cloth in his hand. A split second later, he felt the raging heat erupt over his body as the fuel ignited.

The dragon shook wildly and tried to roll in the snow. The pain was coursing over his skin and sapping his strength. Farthington knew he was in a dangerous situation despite his size and fiery breath. If that microlight had more fuel, or weapons, or the winged woman got that staff into him again, he would most likely die. It's time to flee, he thought, but not before Austerley pays for his crimes.

The dragon leapt towards the motionless figure on the ground and snatched him with one taloned foot. Calandra raced at the beast but was knocked aside by a wing. The microlight took a hard turn at Farthington but a flap of his wings caused the over-wing of the aircraft to lift and flip so that the microlight was forced to the ground. James dived out into the snow and Havers careered with the craft into a large snow bank. I have him, thought Farthington. Time to take him somewhere where I can torment him in peace.

As the beast turned to fly away, he was hit first in his right eye. Ignoring this pain, the dragon started to lift but was then hit by another arrow in his claw, forcing it open. Austerley dropped the few feet to the snow. The beast roared his anger but flew hard, away from Austerley and the island. Kirkgordon, with his left arm strapped hard and straight, watched closely until the dragon was out of sight. Only then did he race over to Austerley.

Indy was face down in the snow and Kirkgordon struggled to turn him over with his one good arm. A quick scan of his colleague showed him to be breathing at least, but his leg was bleeding copiously. A dark red patch of snow, with pinkish tinges at its edges, lay where a foot should have been.

"Cally! Havers! Someone! Get over here!" Kirkgordon was accustomed to seeing injuries, but the foot's absence seemed surreal. He started to slap

Austerley's face.

"Indy! Bloody hell, Indy, speak to me. Wake up!"

"How bad is it, Churchy?" said a breathless Calandra.

"Bad. Bloody bad. I mean, he's breathing but there's too much blood. It needs to be stemmed but my arm's shot."

"Move!" Calandra stepped in front of Kirkgordon. She ripped part of her top off and applied it to the ankle stump. The rag turned red almost instantly.

Kirkgordon sensed someone over his shoulder and turned to see James standing motionless, staring at Austerley. His eyes were cold. Numb, in fact.

"Look away, kid. Look away." The child continued to stare. "James," said Kirkgordon, trying a different tack, "where's Havers?"

James continued staring but threw a directional thumb over his shoulder. Glancing in the general direction, Kirkgordon saw a staggering Havers making a determined track through the snow.

"Havers, are you okay?"

"Mr Kirkgordon, didn't see it all but caught that rather mean shot to the dragon's foot. Good show, sir." Havers was breathing hard but demonstrating the British stiff upper lip to its full effect. "How is our apprentice necromancer? Blimey, where's his foot? We need to pack it in ice."

"You'll need to swim and find it. Farthington ripped it off. It's attached to a piece of board somewhere in the sea, but with all the turmoil it could be well down."

"That's a lot of blood, Calandra dear, I take it it's not clotting at all." Calandra shook her head. "Well, time for an executive decision, I think, or Mr Austerley won't be worrying about walking but rather what kind of wood he wants his box made of."

"He needs a hospital, Havers! Now! How we going to get him to one? It's not like we can just fly out of here. He's going to bleed to death, man. Dammit!" Kirkgordon got to his feet and turned away. He yelled into the dark. "Why? Why? We came. I trusted. I did the dirty work. We stopped them for you. I'm broken. My friend is dying, so where are you? Tell me! Answer me! Where?"

"Mr Kirkgordon! Desist! Right now! Miss Calandra, we are going to need your staff. That trick where you get the end up to a high temperature, I need you to do that now. It's time we sealed Mr Austerley's wound. James, get clothing or sticks, anything that makes a decent dark mark on the snow. We're going to write a message on the ground."

"For who, exactly? Tell me that, Havers."

"Mr Kirkgordon, please remain calm. You are trying my patience. When the door was opened for Dagon to come through, certain associates will have picked up on the, shall we say, spiritual and temporal anomalies that were happening. People are coming. Probably a scrambled fighter from a certain Scottish airfield. An appropriate message will get a helicopter to us and Mr Austerley some treatment.

So if you can't be of assistance then please refrain from such outbursts. Ah, Calandra dear, excellent, it's white-hot."

Kirkgordon collapsed to the ground, exhausted physically, emotionally and spiritually. Dammit, Havers was good. But there were no guarantees. What had turned Austerley round? There was no sense in it. Austerley had been a foot from an arrow in the head. He'd nearly killed him and just now he'd been screaming at the unfairness of his dying. God, you and me need some words, but not now, just not now. Thanks.

A Eurofighter raced through the sky overhead. He heard Havers congratulate James on a job well done. Then Austerley was screaming. White-hot pain or nightmares from the recent past? Kirkgordon lay back. Damn, this snow was cold.

Chapter 31

Havers Holds it Together

His face had those little circles you got from sleeping on a perforated metal bench. A plaster cast with the felt-tip penned inscription "Dagon basher" adorned his left arm. Despite all anecdotal evidence to the contrary, the coffee in the brown plastic cup was not bad at all and had revived him after the nap. Still, Kirkgordon was worried.

Havers had said everything would be okay, as the chopper had arrived in good time and Calandra had done a marvellous job of sealing up Austerley's wound, stopping the rapid blood loss. Certainly the government man had been right about the cavalry arriving. From the moment that Eurofighter had passed overhead, it had seemed that Her Majesty's

Forces were viewing the island as the most important strategic location in the United Kingdom, surpassing even Buckingham Palace.

A Chinook helicopter had landed and taken Austerley, Calandra and himself off to the hospital on the mainland. They had rushed Kirkgordon into a room in the emergency ward where his arm had been assessed and promptly placed into a cast. Calandra had gone with Austerley who had been rushed into the operating theatre. Kirkgordon found her asleep on one of the metal benches, in the open air, just outside the waiting room. She didn't feel the cold and it was stuffy inside, so he had curled up on the bench opposite and gone to sleep too.

When he awoke, Calandra brought Kirkgordon up to speed on the medical staff's most recent report. All they would say was that Austerley had lost a lot of blood and they were doing everything possible. Smiles of sympathy were in full flow but no information followed.

"He'll be okay," said Calandra.

"Let's hope so, eh."

"Don't beat yourself up. You saved him. You damn well saved him."

"I tried to kill him. He might remember that."

"He looked into the face of Dagon, Churchy. I'm just hoping he still has some semblance of a mind."

"Thought you said he'd be all right?"

"Yeah, well, you gotta hope for the best." She gave a tender but nervous smile and started to walk about in small circles. They varied in direction but she never got more than about five paces from

Kirkgordon.

"Anything from Havers at all?"

"He called, looking for you, but as you were flat out I fielded it for you. Said he'll be here soon. In fact, he was en route in a chopper when he called. Apparently there's some tidying up to be done on the island, but he did say he had taken James to his mother. She's good, well, as good as anyone could be after that freak show."

"There's bound to have been a few of the frog-men and fish-heads that got away. Havers will want all that tidied up. Surreal, all that stuff. Austerley played it so damn close. Clever though, he managed to take just about everything into that portal."

"But you called it, Churchy. You said we would do it. You said that thing about Dagon toppling. You had faith."

"I'm not so sure I did. Any word on Farthington?"

"None. I think he's Havers' number one priority. I really don't get the change in him. He was always a typical dragon: gold, gold, gold. If it didn't have money on it, he didn't care. Maybe he was promised something."

"Maybe, or maybe a master just pays well."

Kirkgordon lay down again on the bench and soon drifted off. A combination of tiredness and painkillers were taking the edge off his usual alertness, and it took a good shake from Havers to bring him back out of the dream world.

"Mr Kirkgordon, how is the arm, sir? Damn fine job, damn fine job. Have you eaten? You'll need to eat. On your feet and we'll go down to the canteen for a bite."

"Havers, easy man, just waking up. Anyway, Austerley's still in theatre. Going to be here when he gets out."

"That'll be another hour minimum, so let's get Miss Calandra and yourself fed."

"An hour? How do you know?"

"You don't think Mr Austerley has been entrusted solely to the services of this hospital? They're good people, they work hard and deliver good care but they're not so hot on the protection from hostile forces. My people are here and I am keeping a close eye on Mr Austerley's progress."

"Ah, whatever then. You owe me at least a coffee. More like steak dinner for twenty, actually!"

"Calandra, dear, join us. I'm going to take the hunger pangs off Mr Kirkgordon." It was a standard hospital canteen, clean and bland in décor. The food, while not elaborate, was solid and wholesome. Having demolished haggis, neeps and tatties, Kirkgordon soon finished off a large bowl of spotted dick with ice cream. Due to the lack of a bar, his hankering for a beer was muted down to a fizzy apple drink.

"Were there many of them left, Havers?" asked Kirkgordon.

"We think up to twenty or thirty, but there's a whole battalion of soldiers combing that island. We got most of them. Not quietly either, but with sub-machine guns. Totally different prospect than fighting hand to hand. I knew Calandra could handle herself but you did well too. Pretty decent with the bow. From about six years old, I believe."

"Is there no level of research you don't stoop to?"

"Frankly, Mr Kirkgordon, no. I don't take risks and hence I rarely get caught out." Havers' mind drifted back to James. Rarely, he thought, but I would have been dead without the kid. Scarred him for life too, no doubt. Havers made a mental note to make sure the family was well looked after and to keep an eye on the kid as a potential recruit.

"What's going to happen to the island? Are the locals going to settle back down again? That's going to be damn hard."

"No. They won't."

"Don't blame them, not sure I'd want to go back."

"Oh, some will want to. But they won't be allowed to. That portal still has the potential to be exploited. So, as of an hour ago the island has become one of the new Scottish Danger Areas, suitable only for missile target practice. We're going to blow that portal to smithereens and then dump so much rock on it Godzilla wouldn't be able to make an exit. There's a spiritual darkness there now that we can't get rid of so easily."

"Get a priest then," laughed Calandra.

"What about you, Calandra? Where do you go from here? Back to Russia?" Kirkgordon inquired.

"Hardly. I showed my wings in the café, remember. FSB will want to talk to a woman who can do that, even an cold, old bird like me."

"So what then?"

"Miss Calandra will be under my employ," said Havers. "It's not often I can bring in someone who knows the night so well."

Kirkgordon raised his eyebrows at Cally. She dropped her head slightly then smiled. "It's been invigorating, Churchy, why not? With no man to take care of me, I'd better take care of myself." Kirkgordon smiled. He got the dig, gentle as it was. Different time, different circumstances, different era. He laughed to himself.

The three sat in silence with only the occasional message coming through on Havers' phone. Kirkgordon kept mulling over the last few days but everything came back to him firing that arrow. He was able to get past the killing of the frog-men and fish-men, after all, they had been trying to kill him and plunge the world into eternal darkness. There was at least a decent self-defence plea to be made. But Austerley had been a colleague, if not a friend. Only good fortune, only the difficulty of the shot, had prevented his death. Kirkgordon had aimed to kill, and that was a feeling he had hoped to have buried along with his previous job.

"Mr Austerley has been taken from theatre and is recuperating in a side room. Let's pop in," said Havers.

Circling above him was that accursed dragon. And it had a foot in its mouth, dripping blood. The snow around him was a pinkish red, but the blood kept spreading to darken the outlying ground further. In the distance he could see Dagon, laughing wildly, with Calandra on his shoulders in a leather bikini and in chains. Then came the arrows. They came in from all directions, pinning him to the ground. Except the ground had changed into a board. Then suddenly above him was Kevin Bacon. A young Kevin Bacon. And a tune from a film he had watched in younger days. The actor was dancing, sliding at times to his knees. And the lyric that drove at his head. Everybody cut, everybody cut....

Waking with a start, Austerley's eyes first fixed on Calandra. He just stared, disbelieving. Then he pulled himself up as best he could to the head of the bed and started shouting.

"Is he here? Dagon, where's Dagon? Is he here?"

"No, Mr Austerley, he's gone. He's just in your mind. Relax," said Havers.

"Get her a blanket!" shouted Austerley, looking past Havers at Calandra. All three of his audience looked at him with puzzlement.

"It's okay. I'm fine."

"No, no, it's him. At me again. You're with him, trapped with him. Farthington. All Farthington."

"Nurse!" shouted Kirkgordon. "Nurse, help required." A nurse presently ran into the room and, singularly failing to calm Austerley down, resorted to sedating him.

"I fear it may be sometime before Mr Austerley is quite himself again."

"He wasn't too kosher in the first place," said Kirkgordon. "It's not too far back to his starting point."

"The point is, Mr Kirkgordon, he'll need constant attention, monitoring and protection. I can't commit to that, no matter how valuable an asset he may be."

"Hang on there, Havers. An asset, that's what you see? The man was a happy camper in the loony bin until he got involved in this mess. Now look at him. You owe him. You owe him, big time."

"Maybe, Mr Kirkgordon, but I haven't the resources. Yes, the finances, but not the resources. For a man of such complex and dangerous tendencies, he'll need someone special to protect him."

"Don't go there, I have a family to get back to."

"You owe him too, Mr Kirkgordon, you did try to kill him."

"On your instruction. No, no. There's no way." Not with hope blossoming with Alana.

"Fine, I'll set him free. But when Farthington comes back and Mr Austerley's body is in twenty pieces, you'll not be able to live with yourself."

"And you would, Havers. You damn well would." Kirkgordon thought for a moment. "Havers, here's the deal. I want an apartment, sea view, three bedrooms. I'll look after Austerley part-time, fifty-fifty split. Two weeks on and two off. Your people cover my time off. And I'm on the payroll."

"Naturally. A good compromise. Given all you have seen, if you didn't join up, I'd have to kill you."

"Don't joke, Havers, just say yes."

"Oh, it's a yes. And, Mr Kirkgordon, when exactly was I joking? Although to be fair, I may have used one of my people to do the elimination."

And he's got me, right where he wanted, thought Kirkgordon. God, I hope you know what you're doing.

THE END

G R Jordan

Acknowledgements

To Janet for pushing me ever forward in this writing journey and for believing even when I doubted. To my wonderful children for letting their Dad have some space and letting me be in their story.

To Al, for your encouragement, feedback and being a friend in all this madness. One day we need to jump a fence on a motorbike, the real thing has to be easier!

To Jean, Margaret, and everyone else who has given feedback during the writing, your comments and help are much appreciated.

To Peter Urpeth and Emergents, thanks for the continued support and help.

To Ben Galley, your workshop was a catalyst, thanks for trekking to the wilder parts of Scotland.

To the fantastic American gentleman who misheard my friend's name and then sent a package to a certain Mr Austerley. Your error was a gaff of genius.

To Kathleen and the Stornoway Writer's Group. Thanks for all the encouragement and honesty.

To God who gave me this creative talent, may He
watch over me like He watches over Kirkgordon.

Further Information

I hope you enjoyed this romp around the globe and if you want to hear more about Austerley and Kirkgordon, or more about my writing then please check out the links below. Please do feed back anything you liked, or even disliked, queries, comments or maybe even your ideas for the characters' future.

Website: www.carpetlessleprechaun.co.uk
Twitter: @carpetless
Facebook: http://facebook.com/carpetlessleprechaun
Wattpad: www.wattpad.com/user/GRJordan/about
Goodreads: www.goodreads.com/author/show/8293636
Email: carpetlessleprechaun@hotmail.com

Austerley and Kirkgordon will return in

THE
DARKNESS AT
DILLINGHAM

Lightning Source UK Ltd.
Milton Keynes UK
UKOW02f2242240416

272864UK00002B/7/P